Ro...
A Royal MC Novella

Elle Boon

By Elle Boon elleboon@yahoo.com

Cover art by: Furious Photography

Not every hero wears a cape, my guy Tymber is a hero you'll want as your own! xoxo Elle Boon

Royally Twisted

A Royal MC Novella

Copyright © 2019 Elle Boon

First E-book Publication: 2019

Cover design by Furious Photography

Edited by: Tracy Roelle

All cover art and logo copyright © Furious Photography

PUBLISHER:

Elle Boon

Contents

Dedication

I'd like to dedicate this story to my mama, who is a three-time cancer survivor and is currently battling stage 4 lung cancer, and to all the men and women who have battled with cancer and their families. Cancer is the 2nd leading cause of death in the United States. The number of deaths per year are as follows: 598,038 making the total deaths 21.7 percent.

There's also an underlying story mixed into this that hits home with me. Suicide, no matter what age, is something I wouldn't wish on anyone, yet it affects so many of us, my family included.

Each day, in the United States alone, there's an average of over 3,041 suicide attempts made by young people in grades 9–12. The number of Americans who die by suicide is 44,965 each year. There are 13.8 deaths by suicide per 100,000 persons each year. Almost 500,000 people are treated in emergency rooms each year for self-inflected injuries. These are staggering statistics that I hope can be prevented. Suicide is the tenth leading cause of death in the US, accounting for more than 1% of all deaths with it being the second leading cause of death among people ages 15-24. Eight out of ten people considering suicide give some sign of their intentions.

We can all help to prevent suicide. The **Lifeline** is one way, providing twenty-four hours, seven days a week free and confidential support for people in distress. It provides prevention and crisis resources for you or your loved ones, and best practices for professionals.
The number for Lifeline is; tel:1-800-273-8255

No suicide attempt should be dismissed or treated lightly!

No matter the race or age of the person or how rich or poor they are, most people who die by suicide have a mental or emotional disorder. The most common underlying disorder is depression. Suicide victims suffer from major depression or bipolar (manic-depressive) disorder. That total is a staggering number at 30% to 70%. If you or someone you know is contemplating suicide, call 1-800-SUICIDE (1-800-784-2433) or 1-800-273-TALK (1-800-273-8255).

https://suicidepreventionlifeline.org/
This will connect you with a crisis center in your area.

Love y'all so hard,
Elle

Prologue

Ivy's heart hammered against her chest. Her blood ran cold through her veins at the desperation in Luke's tone as she beat against the bathroom door, praying he'd open up. "Dammit, let me in. Let's talk about this," she begged. Over her shoulder, she glared at the blond man who ruined their carefully constructed world. He shrugged one broad shoulder, seemingly unaffected by what was happening.

A whimper came through, giving her a renewed sense of purpose, giving her hope. How the fuck had things gone from perfectly fine when she'd left home that morning to this...a complete shitshow, she wasn't sure.

"Everything's fucked. I can't face them, Ivy." Luke's voice sounded desperate.

She pressed her palm to the door, leaning her forehead against the hard wood. "Luke, baby, we've gotten through tougher shit, we can get through this."

The man behind her growled, but she waved her free hand frantically, needing him to shut the hell up. Luke tended to be a drama king, only something told her this was different.

"Not this time, love. Not this time. King knows. He knows something. I love you, Ivy. Remember I've always loved you."

She jerked backward at his words, her palms sweating. "Luke, open this fucking door. Stop talking like an idiot, and let's sit down and figure this out."

Time seemed to suspend at the sound she'd heard many times when she'd been at the rifle range, the sound of a shell being inserted and then the barrel being locked in place. Panic had her reaching above her head for the key kept over the frame to unlock the door, fearing she'd be too late, worried she'd piss Luke off. Fear won out as she pushed the key in.

Ivy burst through the door at the same time as the shotgun boomed through the small space. Most people would've been screaming, and maybe she did. Her body jerked as if it too felt the impact of the bullet, her hand going over her mouth. In slow motion, her feet took her the short distance where Luke lay, his eyes staring up at the ceiling, his body in a pool of blood. "Oh god, Luke, what did you do?" she sobbed, shaking, slipping on Luke's blood.

"Holy shit. I'm calling 911."

She heard someone say as if from far away, but she just wanted another moment with Luke before he was gone, but he was already gone, his eyes, those beautiful chocolate eyes, were vacant. "You promised you'd never leave me alone. You lied, damn you." How many times she'd laid on his chest and cried her eyes out, she couldn't remember, but none of them had ever been filled with only her heart beating. "We were going to raise our kids together one day, remember?" Another sob escaped followed by another. Her body felt heavy, the blood was cooling. Shouldn't it stay warm longer? He was her best friend. They'd met in grade school when he'd punched a boy for pulling her pigtails. They'd become best friends when she'd punched a girl for breaking up with him in junior high. They became the *it couple* in high school when he became her…everything. Now, he was lying in a pool of thick, cooling blood.

Ivy stayed there on the bathroom floor with the tangy scent of copper filling every fiber of her being, covering every inch of her body. She was sure she'd never be clean again, but not wanting to leave Luke alone, needing to make sure he had someone with him. Fuck, his brothers were going to kill her was her last thought before she shut down and just floated.

Chapter One

Tymber shook Alan's hand at the end of the meeting. "Thanks for coming and talking tonight," Alan said.

"No thanks needed, man. You and I both know I owe you and this place my sanity. If I can give even a small amount back, I'll do it." He grinned at the raised brow his friend gave him. Sure, back when he'd first began coming to the meetings, he'd only done it to make his sisters happy. Of course, he'd found it an easy way to pick up women, then he'd actually found a little peace in the place. A win win for a man who hadn't had much to look forward to back then. Coming up on his five year cancer free date, he felt a little bit of everything. One of them being the need to celebrate.

He saw a slim form pass by the open door, her dark hair shone in the hallway catching his attention. He was sure he'd seen her walk past a couple times before. He made his excuses and went to see if he could find the beauty, coming to a hard stop outside the door. His brows pulled down into a frown as he watched her stand on her tip toes outside one of the meeting rooms. Although he'd used the meetings in the beginning as his personal pickup place, 'cause seriously, he was a guy who had issues five years ago. Cancer being the biggest one, losing his hair not really much of an issue, but undergoing a mastectomy seriously fucked with his head. He kinda became a dick and used the meetings as his personal playground. Hell, women there had been easy pickings, and he'd been just the dickhead to take advantage. Now though, he didn't like the idea of anyone coming around to spy.

"Think she's lost?" Alan murmured.

"No clue but I'm about to find out." The woman in question had on black combat boots, giving her a couple inches in height, but he could see she was a petite little thing. However, the window was still too high for her to see through without jumping. Tymber didn't think she'd be the type of woman to do such a thing, but he'd been surprised before.

"Isn't that the suicide meeting?"

He glanced back at Alan, giving him a look that said shut the hell up, just as their friend Aubrey strolled out of the back room. "Hey, who're we spying on?" she whispered.

Tymber tipped his head up toward the ceiling and stepped back into the room. She was one of the only ladies he considered a friend and wasn't one with benefits. Again, he was that guy before his diagnosis. Of course, she'd been pregnant when they'd first met five years ago and bent on keeping her child even if it had meant her life. Today, she's a mother to a four year old. She upped her crazy by naming Tymber as one of the kids godfathers. Like him she was in remission and thriving. He'd told her she had to live, or he'd have her kid tatted up by fifteen. "Aubs, you need a filter."

"So says the manwhore. Go see if she needs help getting into the meeting, Tymber," Aubrey gave him a shove.

"Fuck, Aubrey, you can't make someone go to a meeting if they don't want to. Why don't you two go home, and I'll go have a chat. Maybe she's just lost." He winked at the two people who were the complete opposite of him, yet were two of his closest friends, next to Ember and Lincoln at Twisted Ink, the tattoo shop they owned together. "I'll see if I can't help her."

"She doesn't need your D to convince her to not end her life, Tymber," she whispered.

Tymber rolled his eyes. "Did I say she did? What, do you need the D, Aubs? Not mine since that is off the table and all, what with you being like my sister and everything." He grinned at the dirty look she shot him while flipping him the bird.

"Just don't be an ass, Tymber Black," she warned.

It was his turn to flip her the bird as he waited for Alan and Aubrey to leave. He was glad to see the two of them together and happy. Aubrey's fiancé had left her as soon as he'd heard she was pregnant, then after the baby was born, he signed his rights away. If any man was a dick, it was that guy and guys like him.

Walking out the door, he made his way toward the mystery woman, wondering what would make a stunner like her want to kill herself. Her outfit screamed zero fucks given but clearly cost a lot of money. He was the only boy of four and knew enough to spot name brands. Harley Davidson clothes were sexy as fuck but weren't cheap. Paired with the leather mini skirt, and the dollar signs were adding up. The slim, sexy legs he could imagine wrapped around his waist or neck…he truly was an equal opportunity guy, looked as though she worked out.

"You going to stand there all night and eye fuck me, or move on?"

Tymber brought his gaze up, startled to see bright green eyes glaring back at him. Black hair, green eyes, and porcelain skin. Black Irish his mama would've call her. Damn, he bet she had the fiery temper too. "Sorry, I was trying to get the nerve up to speak to you," he lied.

She fell back onto her feet, no longer standing on the tips of the boots she wore, the leather making a creaking noise in the silence of the hall. "Uh huh, and you thought my ass had all the answers?"

A grin split his lips. "Sugar, many a fine ladies' asses have left me speechless, yet none have given me answers. Does your ass talk?"

It was her turn to grin. "Well, I'm told when I walk away men's tongues tend to wag. Does that count?"

He stepped closer, keeping his hands in his pockets, not wanting to appear threatening. Damn, she smelled fucking amazing. "I'd ask for a demonstration, but I find myself not wanting you to leave."

She snorted. "Good line, lumberjack."

Tymber startled at the name. "What?"

"The flannel and work boots. Hence lumberjack. Although I do have to say California is a far cry from the woods." As she spoke, her hand went up and down, outlining his frame, indicating his attire.

He thought about her words, then nodded. "So, going by clothing choice, you'd be goth girl. Oh, we are a pair. The lumberjack and goth girl. Surely those are superhero names or should be."

She laughed, then bit her lip. "I...this is odd."

He moved across the hallway, giving her space when he sensed she needed it. He leaned against the wall, raising one leg up and resting his foot on the wall and then crossed his arms. "Nah, not odd. Ant Man was odd," he said when the silence stretched too long.

Finally, she nodded. "You're right; that could work. Our superhero names," she agreed. "What would be our superpower?" she mimicked his pose.

Running his hand down his short beard a couple times, he tapped his chin as he thought. "Superman has several powers, but his disguise was fucking lame as shit. I'm gonna go with Iron Man."

"I didn't ask which superhero. I said what superpower," she laughed.

Her laugh was deep, making him think of smooth whiskey.

"Yeah, but after giving it some thought, I decided a complete takeover was due," he argued.

Again, her husky laugh filled the hallway. "You're a rule breaker, aren't you?"

Tymber shrugged. "Only when the rules are stupid. Now, before you get your panties in a twist, I'm not saying your rules were stupid."

When she held her hand up and gifted him with another laugh, he swore he'd do almost anything to hear it again and again. "First of all, I didn't give a rule. Second of all, I don't have any panties on." Her cheeks turned a delicate pink, but she didn't break eye contact.

Oh, he liked her sass. Now, he just needed to convince her to go to the suicide help meeting, or maybe he could help her. He knew all about thinking life was over. Five years ago, he was sure his time was up. He'd never heard of a man getting breast cancer. For fuckssake, he didn't have tits like a woman. Sure, he had pecs, he worked out and had muscles, but not huge man boobs. A nice six pack and he felt he was good to go. No, he wouldn't win any body building competitions, but he didn't give a shit about them. He'd had women say they could wash their tongues on his abs…and he'd let them. Ahh, the good old days.

"Hey, you okay?"

Shit, he needed to keep his head on straight.

"My name's Tymber Black, by the way," he blurted.

Big green eyes widened. "Oh, um, I'm Ivy."

He moved off the wall, holding out his hand. "Nice to meet you, Ivy. Would you like to go grab a cup of coffee and discuss our superhero status further?"

Wariness filled her gaze. "Is that a euphemism for lets go have sex?"

Her pale hand trembled in his large one. "Sugar, when we have sex, there will be no euphemisms. I'm not one to worry about being too harsh or blunt. If I have something to say, or if I feel something, I just say it. Life is too short to play those type of games."

19

Ivy looked down at their clasped hands. His tan, rough, work hardened ones with tattoos on them looked so different to hers. Oh, not that she didn't associate with men who had similar looking hands, far from it. Most of the men she knew had plenty of tattoos, only they were big badass men who gave no quarter. She shook her head, clearing it of thoughts of anyone but the gorgeous man in front of her. "Alright," she said before she could stop herself. "Coffee sounds great."

He laughed; the rich sound made butterflies dance in her stomach. "There's a great little place around the corner called The Brew and Sip."

She knew it was probably a bad idea. Probably on the top of her ten worst, but she nodded her agreement. Her hand still clasped in his felt right, which was one hundred percent stupid, so she pulled away. "I'll meet you there," she stuttered, hating how unsure she sounded. Goddamn, where had the cocky girl gone?

"You gonna drive around the block? Come on Ivy Irish, live a little," he implored, smiling, showing a dimple in his right cheek. Tymber reached for her hand again, his touch gentle like he was used to wary women. "I'll keep you safe."

Her heart lurched at those words. The same ones she'd heard dozens of times, only to be shunned. With a force of will her mama said she came out of her womb with, she pasted on a smile, gave his hand a squeeze before breathing deeply. "Lead the way, lumberjack."

"You know that nickname kinda turns me on." He winked. Before she could respond, he began pulling her back down the hall, away from the door that she didn't have the guts to walk through. Next time, she promised herself.

Chapter Two

They walked out the front door, her hand still enclosed in Tymber's. He was a complete contradiction. He dressed like a...well, a lumberjack. Yet he had the manners of a gentleman but talked of sex with her like it was a given. Her body said get it girl, while her mind was throwing up all kinds of stop signs. He was exactly the kind of guy she was attracted to, the kind of man she would've dated. The exact type she should be running in the opposite direction from, instead of holding his hand while they walked to a coffee shop together, thinking about what sex with him would be like. Or at the very least, pumping the fucking breaks. Instead, she was letting him hold her hand and lead her wherever he wanted. Damn, where did the Ivy who'd promised herself she'd make wiser choices go?

"Penny for your thoughts," Tymber's deep voice interrupted her internal struggle.

Ivy did a mental shake. "I was thinking how ironic this is." Which was true. She'd gone to the center looking for a...a what, she wasn't sure. Absolution, solace, a place to vent? Maybe a little of all three, only to chicken out and come face-to-face with a man who made every inch of her wake up and take notice.

He didn't respond as they reached the coffeeshop. The heavenly aroma of fresh brewed beans had her inhaling deeply. "Lord, I love that smell. If I could I'd have it bottled up in a perfume."

Tymber's lips tilted up in a grin, and she just knew what was going to come out of his mouth was going to be dirty. The man didn't disappoint. "Hm, that would definitely wake a man up. Not that I'd need that to wake up around you." He wagged his brows.

She punched his arm playfully. "I get the feeling you don't need help in that department." She looked him up and down, admiring the way he filled out the denim jeans. Damn, he really was built.

Ivy was saved from further comment as they moved to the front counter, placing their orders. Tymber ordered two coffee cake slices, declaring her underfed. Ivy raised her brows, placing her hands on her hips. "Have you the need of glasses, sir?" she questioned him. She was a lot of things, but skinny wasn't one of them. Curvy and proud of it. However, since Luke's death she'd lost a few pounds, but not so much she would be considered skinny.

"I see you perfectly. Every damn inch of you looks perfect to me." Tymber paid for the coffee and the cakes, smiling at the young girl who blushed as he winked at her. "Booth or table?"

She looked at the booth with its padded seats, then the table by the window. "Booth please."

Once they were seated at the booth, he waited for her to settle in before motioning toward the coffee cake. "Alright, try it."

Picking up the fork, she cut a small piece off, bringing it to her mouth. She felt Tymber's eyes on her the entire time, but she forgot about him as soon as the delicious morsel hit her tongue, moaning her pleasure. "Oh my god, this is amazing."

He sat back, a satisfied smile on his too handsome face. "Told you."

She finished chewing, then took another bite before responding. "Aren't you going to try it?"

They both began eating the little treat until their plates were empty. She sat back, smiling as he scraped his plate. "You have a sweet tooth, Mr. Black," she announced, pointing her fork toward him.

Tymber shrugged. "Only when I know its good sweets."

There was no way she could miss his double entendre, or maybe she was reading too much into his words. Hell, maybe it was her who was the horny one, wanting him while he was being the polite guy.

"So, what do you do? I mean for a living that is?" Ivy asked after clearing her throat. Jesus, she sounded like a damn teenager on her first date instead of a grown ass woman who lived a crazy life.

The man across from her picked up his coffee cup, took a sip, then sat it back down. "I own a tattoo shop with a couple buddies here in town."

His words had her sitting up taller. Sure, he looked like a, well a lumberjack with the flannel and jeans, but a tattoo artist was something she wouldn't have guessed. "Oh, which one?" Their city was pretty big, nothing like Los Angeles to the south of them, but Santa Clarita had over two hundred thousand people. She chose the center on the opposite side of town for a reason, the main one being that nobody who ran in her circles would be around, she'd hoped.

"Twisted Ink. It's right off the highway." Pride suffused his tone.

Her heart beat against her chest. She'd heard of his shop. A few of the MC brothers had gotten inked there. Hell, she'd almost gone there herself, only circumstances kept her from going the last time. "That's pretty cool. How long you been doing that?" Just because he tattooed members of the MC didn't mean he would be friendly with them. She'd been around them her entire life and would've seen him if he'd been a prospect or a hang around. No, Tymber hadn't been at any of the club parties or at the clubhouse. Of course, with his intensity, she could see him fitting in just fine with the Royal Sons, no problem. Fuck, she didn't need another MC member in her life.

"What's wrong?" He reached across the table, taking the coffee cup out of her hands.

Ivy hadn't realized she'd picked up the hot liquid or noticed her shaking hands. "Nothing, I just realized how late it was. I should be going." She really didn't want to go. Something about the man sitting so calmly, like a solid tree, made her want to lean on him. She knew that was dangerous territory, because she'd learned not to rely on anyone but herself. To rely on anyone else would only lead to heartache and a letdown. No, she would only trust in herself. Men, especially big tough men like Tymber, like the men of the Royal Sons MC, didn't care about anyone but themselves and their brothers.

She was shocked at the ease talking with Tymber was. The guys she'd been with before were all about themselves, yet here was this gorgeous stranger wanting to know about her and her life. The only problem, or main problem being she couldn't tell him too much, or he'd run for the hills.

For the next hour and a half, two cups of latte and another piece of cake later, Ivy didn't know if the guy was for real or a figment of her imagination. He listened when she spoke yet didn't push when she stopped.

"I don't know what your past relationships were, but from the look on your face, I figure you must've only been with assholes. Ivy, there ain't a man or woman alive who should make you feel as though you were worthless." His gaze ensnared her almost the same as the hand he placed over hers. She wondered if tattoos on his hands, the intricate designs, were meaningful.

"How do you know what my past relationships were like?" she asked, her heart racing. No way had he seen or heard of her before today.

Tymber smiled, not the megawatt, melt the panties off of every woman within his vicinity, but a knowing one that had her pulling her hand back. His words ringing in her ears. He'd change his mind if he knew her past.

"I really should head out. Thank you for the coffee and cakes, although my ass isn't going to be thanking you when we can't wiggle into our favorite pair of jeans," she joked, hoping her tone rang true.

"I'll walk you to your car." Tymber scooted out of the booth before she could protest.

"You don't have to do that. I've been on my own for a long time. I'm pretty sure I can make it back to my car just fine." She looked up into his gorgeous eyes, willing her voice to be strong.

He nodded. "Just the same, I'll walk you to it, if you don't mind."

"And if I mind?" she asked.

He shrugged. "I'll still do it, only I'll be the asshole who walked you to your car instead of the nice man you met."

She laughed. "I have a feeling you really can be an asshole."

The cooler air slapped at them when they walked outside, making her suck in the fresh scent. Silence greeted her words, which gave her a chance to look around the area. A few bikes were parked along the road outside of shops. She didn't recognize any, but fear skated up her spine.

Tymber watched her look around the neighborhood, not missing the shiver that shook her petite frame. Something had the gorgeous woman scared. Something that also had her running to a suicide help meeting. He vowed he'd find out more. There was a mystique to Ivy that called to him on a visceral level. A connection he'd never felt for any other woman, and he'd met a lot of women, but none brought out such a protective side to him that he wanted to wrap her up in his arms and protect her from the world. His sisters would laugh their asses off if they saw him right now. Being the baby with four older females in the family, he'd been brought up to respect the fairer sex. They'd taught him a lot of things. One of his greatest lessons was their body language, and Ivy's was screaming self-defense. Whoever had hurt her, had her running, would have to go through him to get to her.

He saw her glance toward the row of bikes, then saw her shiver again. Shit, was she scared to ride? He and his buddies liked their rides. Although they weren't affiliated with any of the MCs that were all over California, he was friendly with the club that ran a lot of businesses in Santa Clarita. The president and a few others were clients of his. He took another look at Ivy's appearance, thinking of the women who'd come into the shop with King and Duke and the others. Those women appeared in a lot less clothing than Ivy, but that didn't mean Ivy wasn't an old lady of a biker, or a wannabe. Hell, he fucking hoped she wasn't either of those, because he sure as shit didn't want to get into it with the Royal Sons.

They walked back toward the center, her eyes darting around them as if she waited for someone to jump out at them. Tymber couldn't stand it. By the time they rounded the corner, his nerves were frayed, or maybe that was his control. Either way, he came to a stop, pulling Ivy with him. "What the fuck has you so damn scared? What sent you to a suicide meeting only to chicken out, Ivy?" he asked, his voice more of a growl than he wanted.

Her bright green eyes widened. She darted a look around, her tongue coming out to moisten her lips. "I...I don't know what you're talking about. I wasn't going to a...a suicide meeting. I was lost." She looked down when she said the last.

Tymber gave her a little shake. "Dammit, don't lie. This is fucking serious."

She jerked as if he'd hit her. "You think I don't know that? You think I don't know what is and what isn't serious? Let me tell you what's serious, Tymber." She poked him in the chest. "Walking into your apartment to find your best friend arguing with their boyfriend. Seeing the desolation on his face, the utter defeat stamped on every feature, and then watch as he locked himself in the bathroom. Imagine hearing him crying, telling you he loves you but that he can't do it anymore. Have you ever heard the sound of a gun cocking, the way it echoes in a small space? I have. It's a sound I hear night after night, along with the last words he said before a single shot rang out," she sobbed.

He pulled her into his chest, holding her shaking body against his, absorbing her words. What the fuck? Her best friend was a dude who'd killed himself over a breakup or some shit. "I'm sorry, Ivy. So damn sorry." Shit, nobody deserved to witness something like that.

Her tears soaked his shirt while she cried. Tymber kept one hand on the back of her head, the other he ran up and down her back, murmuring words he couldn't recall if asked. How long they stood on the street like that he had no clue. Finally, she sniffled, the sound almost cute. "I got your shirt all wet," she mumbled.

He almost made a sexual reference but stopped himself. "That's alright, it washes."

"That was hard, wasn't it?" she questioned, leaning back slightly to meet his eyes.

Tymber raised a brow. "What was?"

Ivy wiped the tears away. Her chest rose and fell with her deep inhale. "I could see the wheels turning in your mind. You normally would've made a sexual quip right then but didn't want to be an asshole."

He chuckled at her astuteness. "Do I get points for not saying anything?"

She tried to step back, but his hold prevented her from moving too far. "You get points for a lot, one being the restraint you showed then."

"I'm sorry about your friend," he said, his heart aching for her loss.

"He was my best friend since kindergarten when he beat up a boy for pulling my pigtails." She smiled at the memory.

If he'd been in class with Ivy back then, he'd have done the same. "That's the mark of a good best friend for sure."

"Luke claims I became his best friend when I punched Sally, after she dumped him in junior high because he found out she only wanted to get closer to his brothers."

An image of a younger version of Ivy beating another girl made him smile. "I'd have paid to see that." And he would. The thought of this sassy woman knocking the shit out of another would be hot as hell in his mind.

"I fell in love with him that same year when he beat my stepdad up after he tried to…well, anyway, that was when we became a couple." Her voice cracked.

His mind came to a halt. He wasn't following, or he was missing vital parts to the story. "Ivy, I'm not on the same page. Who are we discussing?"

Her green eyes were shiny with her tears. "Luke. My best friend. My first love. He's…or rather he was gay. We figured it out in high school, but I still loved him, and he still loved me. Our relationship wasn't like, that. I protected him, and he protected me. Only I didn't protect him in the end. I should've known. I should've been there. If only I'd have—" she sobbed.

Tymber gripped the back of her hair, tipping her face up to his so she had to see him when he spoke. "Ivy, I don't know who Luke was. I don't know why he did what he did. What I do know is this. He pulled that trigger, not you. You have survivors' guilt, which is very common I'm told. People say that when someone commits suicide life goes on. What they don't understand is that life is forever changed for those left behind. Many times, suicide is a permanent solution for a temporary problem. I'm not saying that was your friend's issue. Hell, I know nothing of your life or his, but what I do know is that it wasn't your fault. It wasn't the boyfriend's fault either."

She shook her head. "You don't understand."

Staring up at Tymber, she soaked in his words, wishing they were true, wishing Luke's family agreed. God, she wished she believed them to be true. What she knew for a fact, and without a shadow of a doubt, was her life was forever changed and not for the better. Luke had been more than just her friend, they were family. His family had been her family. They'd allowed her to be a part of them only because of him. Now that he was dead, they blamed her. They thought Darian was her boyfriend and that Luke had offed himself because he couldn't stand life without her in it. God, it was so fucked up. "I really wish I could believe that was true. I wish everyone else thought the same way, too."

The feel of his hand gripping her hair, sent a tingle of awareness through her body, reminding her she was still alive, that she still had needs. It had been too damn long since she'd thought of herself as a sexual being. Hell, with her playing the part of Luke's beard, she couldn't just go out and find a guy to scratch the itch. Truth be told, she'd not actually had a boyfriend other than Luke, and well, that hadn't worked out. "I should go," she whispered, but didn't step away.

His grip didn't ease. "Can I get your number?" he asked.

His words were an invitation. She knew it, and he did too. She licked her lips. For one moment in time, she wanted to forget, wanted to escape reality and pretend all was right in her world. Tymber Black looked like the type of man who could help her do just that. "Where are you going?" she asked him instead.

Tymber looked up and down the block. "Home, to my place."

"If I give you my number, are you going to call me if I don't go home with you now?"

Ivy was aware she was taking a huge leap of faith. He was a virtual stranger. Hell, nobody even knew where she was or would even care, but she tossed her proverbial last fuck in the air and nodded. "Want some company?"

He gave a slight tug to her hair, reminding her he had control. "You sure?"

Her mouth had gone dry, but she nodded. "Very," she agreed.

"Want to ride with me?" He pointed toward his bike.

She swallowed, noticing his ride. Just because he rode a bike didn't mean he was part of an MC. She'd never seen him around the Royal clubhouse or around any of the guys. "I'll follow you." Her own bike was parked in the garage behind her apartment.

"Where's your car?"

Ivy pointed to where her 1974 orange Ford Bronco sat. "Right there."

"Dayum, girl. That's a sweet ride. Is it a six speed?" he asked, walking over to peer inside.

"Yeah, but it's been modified. I've pretty much replaced everything under the hood, so it's all brand new, right down to the six point roll cage."

Tymber whistled. "You did the work?"

Ivy rolled her eyes. Men couldn't wrap their head around a female who liked to work on cars and trucks. She was that girl. The one who could and would take an engine apart and put it back together even better than it had been. Case in point, her Bronco. She and Luke had found it sitting in a junk yard up in Sacramento years ago. Slowly, but surely, she'd rebuilt and replaced everything until she had what sat on the road today. The fact she and Luke would never be putting anything back together almost brought her to a crying mess, again. "I had help," was all she said.

His phone ringing had him stiffening. "I need to take this."

She stared as he pulled the little phone out, his jeans hugging him in all the right places. No matter how hard she tried, tearing her eyes away from his back was near impossible. What kind of person does that make her, drooling over a man, thinking of going home with said man she'd met at a crisis center? For all she knew, he too was a suicide survivor. Would being with her cause him more grief?

"Carly, calm the fuck down. I'm sure it's fine. Yeah, I'll be right there." Tymber ran his hand through his hair, turning to look at her over his shoulder. His heated stare conveying more than words could.

Was this the universe's way to tell her she was crazy to go back to his place, with a man she didn't know? Her mind caught up to what he'd said or rather didn't say. She was sure they'd discussed significant others, but here he was promising some faceless woman named Carly he'd be right there. The flex and bunch of Tymber's muscular ass when he pushed the cellphone back into his back pocket was truly enough for most red-blooded women to lose their mind. "I lost my mind years ago, no reason to question its lack of existence now, Ivy Girl," she told herself. If he had a girlfriend, or whatever, she'd find out and walk away now, rather than later after she'd made another mistake.

"I don't think you've lost anything, Ivy. Maybe you've forgotten or misplaced it somewhere along the way."

Chapter Three

Tymber wasn't sure what had made Ivy retreat from him, but he'd be damned if he allowed it. There was something about the woman who was dressed to kill, yet her demeanor was that of a woman in need of saving. He watched and waited for her to process his declaration.

Ivy let out a deep breath. "You should get going. It sounds like Carly is in need of you."

He almost smiled, only knowing Ivy might just kick him with those black boots kept him from following through with it. Nope, he definitely wasn't going to crack a shit-eating grin, even though he understood why she was backing away. Jealousy was a bitch, one that he didn't usually like seeing on a woman he wanted. However, with the gorgeous Ivy, he found he liked it. "My sister tends to go into theatrics when one of her offspring is being a little hard to handle. Hence the frantic call. My nephew is giving her fits," he explained.

Wariness clouded her gorgeous green eyes. "You better get going then." She tilted her head toward his bike.

"You gonna give me your number?" He ran the back of his fingers down her cheek, the softness of it making him wish they'd had more time together. If she didn't give him her number, he wasn't sure how he'd track her down. Of course, he could call a friend who could run her plates, but that would only cause him grief, sure as shit his buddy would demand he explain before he'd run them. How would he explain the crazy need to see Ivy again, to make sure she was safe and happy? Shit, maybe it would be better if she denied him her digits.

"What's your number?" Ivy asked instead.

His brows rose, then he rattled off his number, thinking she'd never call. Ivy pulled her phone out of her bag, typing in his number. He figured she'd delete it once she was away from him. The sound of his phone ringing made the grin he'd fought earlier appear. He slipped his cell out of his back pocket, keeping his eyes locked on hers. "Hello?" he said into the phone, hoping it was Ivy, hating the thought it wasn't.

Silence met his words. Ivy let out a deep breath. "There's my number."

Tymber quickly added her to his contacts. "You've got mine too. Are you going to answer if I call?"

Ivy laughed. "You act as though women turn you down, Tymber. If they have, then you're either a dick once they get to know you, or you have a small dick, which for the record I'm not asking, just saying."

He stepped closer to Ivy, her tongue peeking out to lick over lips he wanted to do the same to. "I can't say I've never been a dick, but I can assure you the size of my dick has never been an issue, except that it might be too big. However, I'm a patient man so even those complaints I can erase."

Her throat worked as she swallowed. "Good to know."

"I'll call you tonight." He made it a statement. If she didn't answer, he wouldn't stalk her or call again.

"My phone will be on. See you, lumberjack." She moved back, then rounded her vehicle, leaving him alone on the sidewalk.

"Yeah, you will," he promised her. Shit, he needed to have his head examined, he thought while watching her tail lights disappear around the corner. Walking over to his bike, he grabbed the skull cap he never rode without and strapped it on. The familiar rumble of the bike usually eased his mind, giving him a respite from reality. However, the vision of Ivy standing on her toes outside a meeting for suicide survivors and those who were on the edge kept him from shutting down. "After I deal with Carl, I'll call her. If she doesn't pick up, I'll leave a message, but then the ball would be in her court," he muttered while easing into traffic.

"Carly, you need to be consistent with the kids. You can't give them their way one day, then expect them to not be pissed when you deny them the next. If you don't want Carl hanging out with certain friends, letting him go to a party with them last week, yet telling him he can't be friends with them isn't going to sit well." He took the cold bottle of water his sister held out. He was thirty-two to her forty-five. Times like this made him wonder how she'd gotten through life without falling flat on her face.

"Tymber, there are reasons for everything. For one, the party I let my fifteen year old son go to last week was being monitored by adults. This one isn't. Hell, the kid he wanted to go with drove a sportscar like a...teen let loose for the first time. I didn't want to see my son get in with him. I don't know how to explain it, but I have a feeling he wasn't going to come home. Call it mother's intuition, but that's what I got."

He walked around the kitchen counter and pulled his sister into his arms. Like him, she had dark brown hair and brown eyes. In her mid forties, she was in better shape than most women in their twenties, keeping her mind and body fit was her way of saying fuck off to her ex. "I don't question your motives, sis. I just hate seeing you upset like this. Where's CJ at?" His nephew was Carl Junior, but he hated when people called him that. Why his sister had married the douche Carl, making them that couple with matching names, he would never know. Their twenty year marriage had fallen apart three years ago, after Carly found out he'd been screwing around on her for the last five years. He wondered if the man had never not cheated but didn't say that to Carly. After all, Carl Senior was now spending a fifteen year jail sentence, thanks to his fall from grace and into the arms of a junkie who set him up. Karma was a bitch, but when she came calling, snaring Carl in a sting operation, nobody in his family cared.

"He's in his room sulking. I tried to talk to him, but he wouldn't open the door, and he's not returning my calls or texts," Carly said, hurt filling her tone and demeanor.

Back when he'd been a teen, throwing a hissy fit like CJ would've been the last thing he would've done. He made his way down the hallway after assuring his sister he'd talk with her son. Shit, he wondered when he'd become the wise one, then gave a chuckle. At CJ's door, he could hear the pounding beat of heavy metal. Two sharp raps on the door didn't elicit a response, but unlike his sister, he wouldn't allow a little thing like that to keep him out. Reaching above the door to his sister's room he found the key she kept there. "I hope you're decent and not jacking off to online porn," he muttered as he opened the door.

"Hardy har har, Uncle Tymber. What did my mom do, call you in for reinforcements?" CJ asked, without turning to look toward the door.

"Something like that," he agreed. Never would he lie to the boy, if he could help it.

"Well, you can go on back to her and let her know I'm being a good little boy. See…" He moved aside to show Tymber what was on the screen. Not that he'd actually thought the kid would be watching porn...but seeing some document he'd been working on had him relaxing.

Tymber walked the few feet from the door to where his nephew sat. Leaning against the desk, he faced CJ. "You know your mother only has your best interest in mind when she gives an order."

"Well my best interests weren't to be kept from going to Dillon's party just because his parents weren't home. It's like she doesn't trust me." Sadness wafted from the boy. Having your dad locked up for drug trafficking and a mother who kept the apron strings too tight had to be hard.

He spent a half hour with CJ, looking over his paper and explaining what could happen if the party was busted. Even though he was sullen, he agreed he didn't want to be anywhere near the police, especially with his father's name still floating in the air. His sister had been lucky when she'd finally divorced the man, or he would've drug her and their children down the rabbit hole he was in.

The kitchen was empty, but he knew where he'd find Carly, by the pool with a book and a glass of water with lemon in it. He shook his head as he stepped out the patio door, taking in the serene picture of the sun setting and the crisp clean air.

"I just got a text from CJ. I guess your talk did him good?" She lifted the glass and took a sip, laying the book down on her lap.

"Yeah, he's still mad but he understands you were only looking out for him. You might want to talk to him before the yelling, you know." He sat on the lounger across from her, his elbows resting on his thighs, waiting.

"Tymber, you can't always be their friend when you're the parent. I guess I could've talked him through my reasoning instead of grounding him, but damn, the boy knows how to push my buttons," she growled.

Oh, he knew all about pushing a parent's button, especially a mothers. Before they'd lost their mom to breast cancer, he'd always pushed buttons or envelopes, whatever he could, to get his way. Hell, at thirty-two, there wasn't much he hadn't done that he wanted. "You don't owe the kid a reason. A little respect goes a long way. Remember, he's a straight A student and has goals. Trust him enough to talk with him before you start the yelling. And while I'm doling out advice, may I suggest you not do it via text?" He lifted his chin toward the pink phone on the table.

Carly blinked, her eyes swimming with tears. "It's hard, Tymber. I only want what's best for him, but he acts like I'm the worst mother in the world when I don't let him have his way. Throwing up his grades doesn't make it okay for him to go to a party with no chaperones."

Tymber agreed with Carly. He hoped his nephew truly did acknowledge his mom only did things for his wellbeing. "I gotta go." He stood up, hugging Carly as she too stood.

"Thanks for coming up and putting out my fires," she joked.

Seated on his Harley as he headed toward his own home, he thought of Ivy and her reasoning for being outside a meeting but not going in. All through their little coffee…he couldn't really call it a date, but it was something, something he wanted to explore further.

Ivy recognized Darian's car outside the flat she shared with him and Luke. Her heart twisted in her chest, making it hard to breathe. "Get your shit together, girl," she muttered then winced. Whenever she'd been nervous or upset, she'd always talked to herself, except when Luke had been there, which looking back, had been almost her entire life. Now, he was gone, and there was this huge hole where he had been in her life, making her feel as though she were swimming against the current. The saying about life isn't finding shelter in the storm, it's about learning to dance in the rain flittered into her mind. "That's what I'm going to get inked on me." It felt as though all she'd done is let the rain that was her shitshow of a life wash her away, instead of standing tall with an umbrella over her head telling the storm to do its worst.

She shoved the door to her Bronco open, making her way to the entrance of where her life seemed to be left hanging. Inside, she climbed the steps to the upstairs apartment. Her boots sounded loud in the empty hallway, but she'd never been one to walk quietly. The sight of the door left ajar sent fear down her spine. With her phone in one hand, she pushed the door open with her foot. "Darian, you home?"

A noise from the living room had her moving as silently as she could. "I've already called 911," she lied.

Darian lifted his head up from the leather sofa, his hand holding his nose that looked as though he'd been in a fight. "You're such a bad liar, Ivy." His words were muffled by the towel he held to his face.

Bruising around both eyes had already appeared. "What the fuck happened here?" The apartment seemed to have been trashed, like those after a weekend bender. Not that she or Luke had ever had one of them at the apartment, but she'd been to enough parties the Royal MC had thrown. Only the damage looked more deliberate than what would happen during a party.

"Some of the Royal Sons showed up and didn't like to see me here. Shit, this is the last thing I wanted or needed in my life. Luke—" He choked up.

Moving to sit next to him, she paused and retraced her steps and shut the door, swearing when her eyes landed on the busted door. "Those fuckers broke the door down?" she asked, sitting down next to him.

"I came home to find them already here. I guess they wanted inside enough, even a locked door wouldn't keep them out." He pulled the towel away from his nose.

"Good lord, you need to get that fixed. It looks broken." Her hand reached for the bloody towel.

"Aren't you scared I'll infect you with my gay blood?" Darian let her take the towel away. "I now understand why Luke didn't want to come out to the club. Fuck, if I could've, I'd have walked away from him years ago. I loved him, Ivy. Why wasn't I enough to keep him from…" His words that were left unsaid broke her heart.

"Darian, listen to me. You weren't the problem, and neither was Luke. The MC may accept many things, but he didn't think they'd allow him to come around, even though his brothers are the Prez and his VP. Hell, the entire MC was created by his family like a hundred years ago. Luke was scared to lose his brothers, whether they be of blood or cut." That was one of the reasons she'd agreed to pretend to be his girlfriend all these years. Luke thought he'd only be accepted if he had an old lady. He didn't want to be a full-fledged member, not like his brothers, yet he didn't want to be cut off from them either. Life had really fucked with him, but she'd loved him.

"I'm moving back home," Darian whispered.

She jerked back, taking in her best friend's boyfriend's appearance. He was a blond Adonis, with his blue eyes and muscled physique. "You mean, home to Iowa?"

Darian nodded, tossing the bloody rag onto the leather ottoman that served as the coffee table. "Are you being rash? I mean, yeah, this place is a mess, but I'm sure they won't be back." If the MC wanted to make a statement, beating the shit out of Darian was it. She hoped. Damn, she hated the uncertainty her life had become.

"I came out here for Luke. I like my job at Pump, but it's not what I planned for my life. Look at me. I'm a twenty-five year old, living with my boyfriend's supposed girlfriend, in the place he took his life. Every day I wake up, wishing it were a bad dream, a nightmare that I could wake from, only to find it's my new reality. I can't stay here and keep my sanity. I was actually packing before I went out to grab something to eat. When I came back to find two men in leather vests tearing shit up, I yelled at them. How stupid was that?" His blue eyes implored her to understand.

"Did they ruin any of your stuff?" she asked, not wanting to get into what had happened. Luke's death was too fresh of a wound for them to talk about. However, she thought at least one person would be able to understand what she was going through. An image of Tymber appeared, his openness made her wish she had met him before.

"Nah, nothing that can't be replaced. Ivy, it's not safe for you here. I think I was a warning to you." He reached for her, taking her by the shoulders and giving her a firm shake. "Are you listening to me?"

"I know the MC, unlike you, Darian. I grew up with them, had my first beer with them. Trust me, they're just blowing off steam. It's been over a month since Luke—since that night. When do you leave?" she asked changing the subject. Her internal alarm for danger was blaring. If the MC decided she were to blame, her very life could be on the line.

"I already booked my flight. There's nothing here except my clothes I want. I'll help you clean up." He stood abruptly, picking up the bloody towel and swore. "I get why he didn't want to tell the entire club, but why not his own brothers? For that matter, how the fuck didn't they know he preferred dudes to women?"

Ivy knew how, and that was why she felt so much guilt. Maybe if she'd encouraged him to be honest with King and Duke, they might've accepted his sexuality. She pictured King Royal, the president of the Royal Sons MC. Her hand flew to her chest as an image of his angry face came to mind. "I should've made him tell King."

"That would've been fun to see, Ivy Girl. Listen, why don't you come with me? My family would welcome you with open arms, and you could start over." He didn't look up as he spoke, his intent to clean up the mess left by the assholes making him grunt in pain from their beating.

"Yeah, that would be the day. Imagine me on a farm in the middle of Iowa. I'm pretty sure the place would flip on its head if I went with you. Besides, this is my home." She gestured toward the mess. Yes, Luke and she shared the place, but it was her name on the lease. "Plus, I just graduated. How many jobs do you think are in Iowa waiting for the likes of me?"

Darian looked her up and down, stopping once he met her eyes. "You could tone down the badass biker chick. You're gorgeous, smart, and way too good for the jerks who did this."

"Let's just clean this mess up. I'll help you get your stuff together." Her mind already on the tasks at hand. Replacing some of the broken pieces would be put on the back burner. Her fingers flew to her mouth. "Did they go into the bedrooms?" Her body jerking as she walked down the hallway toward her room, the one across from Luke's and Darian's.

"No, they must've just gotten in before I walked in on them. At first I thought you'd come home, so I yelled for you. I think that was a big fat match to their flame. I didn't have time to do anything except yelp when one of the big fuckers grabbed me by the neck, shoving me inside the door."

Ivy and Darian worked through the rest of the evening, filling five large garbage bags with trash and things Darian said he no longer wanted or needed. Her hand brushed over the clothing left in the walk in closet, the familiar scent of Luke's cologne tickled her nose. When Darian sighed, she'd looked up to see the pain he couldn't erase from his busted up face. "I'll see you again," she whispered. She wasn't sure if she meant Darian or Luke, only knew her world was being rocked again. Fucking Royal MC and their bastard ways.

It was close to midnight. The apartment was silent, save for the ticking of the clock on the wall. Her mind wouldn't settle. Fear no longer something she seemed to feel. Everyone she'd cared about was gone now that Darian had left. "How pathetic, the only men in my life had loved each other, leaving me on the outside looking in." That had been her life growing up. Luke was her angel when she'd needed him. His loss had a sob escaping before she could quell it. Her body moved on autopilot, making sure the newly replaced door was locked with three sets of deadbolts. It would be a hell of a lot harder for the Sons to break down a steel door with deadbolts like she had installed. Luckily, she knew of a locksmith who also replaced doors, his grey hair had looked like he'd stuck his finger in a light socket, resembling Albert Einstein, but he'd been fast and efficient, everything she'd needed. He'd looked at the door then her, shaking his head, but didn't say anything more until the new door was in place. She had to bite her tongue to keep from telling him to mind his business, only holding the sharp retort in because he truly appeared genuine in his comments and suggestions.

Like she needed him, or anyone, to tell her to lock all three locks and to not open the door unless she knew who was on the other side. Now, hours later, that same door taunted her. If she and Luke would've had the door a month ago, maybe just maybe, he'd still be alive. Instead, he and Darian had been making out on the couch when King had strolled in. She shuttered imagining what the big man had looked like in that moment. Luke said he and Darian hadn't been caught outright, but he worried King or Duke would find out. "Why didn't

I convince him to come out?" she asked, banging her head against the wall. The pain from the impact didn't stop her from doing it again.

Getting up, she triple checked the locks, then walked down the hallway, hating the emptiness of the apartment and her heart. Tomorrow, she'd see about a new place to live.

Chapter Four

"What do you think?" He held a mirror out for King to take. The big son of a bitch didn't have a lot of open canvas on his body, but Tymber had taken the art already there as a layer beneath what he was putting on him. The end result was kickass, in his opinion. Luckily the president of the MC agreed, his dark eyes taking in the two clasped hands holding a rosary with the words *Brothers Forever. Even In Death*, written along the cross that hung from the praying hands.

"Looks great, man. Thanks for getting me in at the last minute." King shrugged into his leather cut, his dark eyes not missing anything. "If you ever need anything, give me a holler." He held his hand out, shaking Tymber's.

"I appreciate that. I don't need to give you aftercare instructions, do I?" he asked, shaking his head at the absurd notion. The other man had almost as many tattoos as he did.

"I'm good. See you around," King stated, his hand releasing Tymber's. "Remember what I said. You need anything, give me a holler. The Sons will come without a question."

Tymber agreed to call if the need ever arose. In the back of his mind, he contemplated what could happen that he'd need the help of the club. He knew about patches and their significance, which was how he knew King was the president. Not seeing a 1% patch on the cut didn't mean they weren't an outlaw club, it just meant they didn't announce it to the world, or he missed it. Nobody could ever say he was a fool, and only a fool would've asked a member of the Royal Sons MC if they were or not. He preferred to keep his head attached to his unbeaten body, thank you very much. Not that he was scared to take on any of the club members one on one. However, he was pretty sure if you fucked with one, you fucked with them all. He hadn't survived fucking breast cancer, only to get his ass handed to him by one of the brothers.

"You look like your contemplating a big problem. Want my advice?" King asked from the doorway.

He had to shake himself to pull his mind back to the present. "Hit me with it."

King chuckled. "Never tell a brother to hit you, he just might. Whatever is bugging you, don't let it consume too much of your time," King warned.

Tymber watched through the window as King got on his Harley, the bike rumbling to life seconds before he pulled out into traffic, several other bikes falling in line behind him. Yeah, he wouldn't forget the other man's words.

A text dinged from where he'd left his phone. Tymber ignored it while he locked up the front of the shop. He cleaned up his station, then gazed around at the space. Besides him and his two partners Ember and Lincoln, they had three other artists who worked for them plus a receptionist. This late at night, it was just him, and he could appreciate all they'd achieved, the three of them, after leaving the military. None of them left the place dirty or cluttered, something that had been drilled into them while in bootcamp. However, he wasn't a fresh faced eighteen year old with a chip on his shoulder anymore. After five years, he'd known the life of a soldier wasn't his. Between the three of them, they bought the location where their shop was located, creating a business he was proud of. There was an apartment above the shop that each of them had used at different times, like tonight when he didn't feel like riding the fifteen miles to home. Bone tired was what he felt.

After he reassured himself the place was locked up, he shook the gate that they'd installed along the front of the room, making sure it was secure. If vandals tried to break in through the glass front, they wouldn't be able to get through without having to go through the locked gate as well.

He picked up his phone, raising one brow at the text. "Who do you think you are, my daddy," he mumbled, his fingers flying over the keys while he headed toward the back. The immediate text back had him chuckling. He pressed the call button for Lincoln instead of responding via text.

"What up?" Lincoln's deep voice echoed down the line.

"I don't know, you tell me. You got cameras in the shop I don't know about?" He entered the code into the lock at the top of the stairs, glad they'd had the foresight to install one that didn't require a key.

"Shit, I don't need to watch you to know what's going on. The motion sensors alert me when someone walks across the threshold. From there, I just pull up the app from the security company, just like you could. I didn't know you were working late?"

He explained about the appointment with King and how the other man had wanted the piece done yesterday, which in Tymber's world meant right that minute.

"You better stay on their good side," Lincoln warned.

"Thanks ma, I surely will do just that," he said in a fake drawl, before locking the door behind him.

A nightlight glowed from one of the outlets, but the curtains in the front were open, allowing light from the streetlights and the moon to illuminate the space.

"I'm glad to hear you're taking this shit seriously. I'll be in the shop early, want me to bring you some breakfast?" Lincoln was one of his best friends, his warning coming from the heart rather than him just being a jackass.

Like him, Link had both arms tatted up along with his back. However, Tymber's chest now sported a huge piece over his scar, blending it in with the artwork. Some days he didn't think about what he'd have done if he'd not found out he had the big C word so early. More than likely he'd be dead instead of standing in the middle of the apartment listening to Link mumble. "Shoot me a text when you're on the way. If I'm still here, I'll take you up on that," he agreed, hanging up after a few more words.

Tymber made his way to the bedroom he used and looked at the clock beside the bed, its bright light of the numbers swam in his vision. "Fuck, I'm whipped." He pressed a button on top, dimming the lights. He was going to sleep for the next twelve hours. His eyes caught onto the last numbers that had called him. Link, King, and Ivy. Just saying her name had his thumb hovering over the keys to call her. Without giving himself a chance to back out, he pressed the call button, waiting for either Ivy's voice, or the voicemail to pick up. It was after midnight, so he wouldn't presume she'd be up, but he wanted to hear her voice. After doing the memorial piece for King, his mind was a jumbled mess. Hearing a sleepy Ivy answer had his dick jerking in his jeans.

"Hey, lumberjack, what's going on?"

Her tone wasn't one of anger at his call so late, which gave him hope. "I just finished doing a tattoo and thought I'd see if you were still up."

The sound of fabric shifting had him imagining her in bed, nekkid. If only he was there to see for himself. Instead, he stripped his shirt off while holding the phone out. Next he stripped out of his jeans, letting them lay where he dropped them. Her deep breath through the phone met his announcement.

"I want a tattoo of a quote. Do you have any appointments open, or maybe one of your other artists could do it?"

Tymber climbed in bed, his instant denial never spoken. If Ivy wanted a tattoo, it would be him inking her perfect skin, not anyone else. "What do you have in mind?" he asked, getting comfortable while she spoke. "Words on a body can be tough. Do you want to write it out and I use it to make a stencil, or do you trust me and my writing?"

"I have shit for penmanship. How's yours?"

Again, the sound of her shifting around made all kinds of thoughts swirl in his brain, but he ruthlessly pushed them back. "How about this. Tomorrow, you come down to the shop, and we'll figure it out?" The thought of seeing her again shouldn't excite him as much as it did. Fuck, he'd never really wanted or needed to see a woman the next day, not even ones he'd somewhat dated. His mind ground to a halt. Had he been a dick all this time he'd considered himself one of the good guys? Mentally he shook the thought away. He was always upfront with women, never led them to believe he was the forever kind.

"I can do that. I, uh, I have some errands to run in the morning. What time is your last appointment?"

Ivy chewed on her thumb nail, the taste of acrylic filling her mouth when she bit too hard, breaking off a piece of her pretty nail color. Another errand she'd have to do tomorrow, or rather later today since it was almost one in the morning. Tymber gave her the time he'd be free, his tone not giving away to how he felt about seeing her again. Taking a huge leap of faith, she told him she'd see him at six the following evening. Before she could hang up, she heard him speaking.

"What did you say? Sorry, I was distracted." Shoot, even to her own ears that was a lame excuse.

"No worries. I was just wondering if you wanted to grab dinner afterward?"

Was that hope in his words or her wishful thinking? Either way, she was grabbing onto his offer with both hands. They talked for another half hour, his quick wit made her laugh more than she'd done in forever. Tomorrow, she'd get the words she'd thought of earlier inked on her ribs, then dinner with the sexy lumberjack.

"See you later," Tymber said.

"Alright, sweet dreams." Good God Almighty, what the hell made her say that? She squeezed the phone in her palm, her eyes closing while she mentally berated herself.

"I sure hope they are," Tymber agreed.

Her death grip relaxed as a laugh tumbled from her. He hung up without another word, but her mind wouldn't shut down quite so easily. Damn, she was so off her game it wasn't funny, coming on to a man she barely knew like she had. "Oh well, what do all the cool people say? Yolo, motherfuckers." Ivy's laugh ended as she thought of Luke and his love of the YOLO way of living. He'd even had it inked on his body, only to have it covered up a few months later. "Such a silly man," she whispered, wishing he were there to tell her what she should wear on her date with Tymber.

*****

The next day she got up, feeling somewhat refreshed after taking a quick shower, and assessed the apartment. Whoever the club had sent over hadn't done any real damage, more of a message sort of thing. Why they were fucking with her, she didn't know. Her entire life had been with the club in some form. First, as Luke's friend, then as Luke's girlfriend. She'd never had a cut like some of the old ladies, the women who wore the patch declaring them the property of whatever brother she was with. Luke hadn't wanted to be like his brothers, yet he was immersed in club politics just the same. It was easy to go along with him as his girl. Nobody fucked with her when she was with Luke. Looked as though that time was over. She wondered if she should call King and find out what was what. An image of him beating the hell out of someone he'd considered a traitor to the club kept her from following through.

Nope, she would ride this out like she did every other pothole in her life. Going from her mother's home to Luke's after her stepdad had tried to get into her bed, Ivy had cried to Luke about the abuse she'd already suffered at his hands. Allowing the fucker access to her bed wasn't something she had been willing to do. Memories flooded her of how her mom had reacted to Ivy's claims. Her hand went to her cheek, the sting from the slap she'd gotten still hurt all these years later. She didn't know if her mother and the jackass were still together. What she did know was that King and Duke had a come to Jesus talk with them both after Luke gave her stepdad a beat down, and then they'd come back with a couple bags of her clothes, promising she'd always have a home with them. "I shouldn't have let Luke talk me into pretending." No use crying over spilled milk, she thought.

After getting ready, she picked up her bag, making sure the new keys were on her keychain, then headed toward the door. A quick glance at the screen showed her the front of the building, assuring her nobody waited at the bottom for her.

Hours later, her palms were sweating while she backed into a spot in front of Twisted Ink. Mentally she prepared herself to see Tymber, yet no amount of preparation could've helped her at her first sight of him, bent over a body with the tattoo gun in his hand. Metal music playing made her entrance less noticeable until the bells above the door dinged, signaling her arrival. Three men lifted their heads, each one previously intent on their tasks. Ivy waved, her eyes caught and held by Tymber's. Damn, the man is even more gorgeous than she remembered. Today, he had on a black T-shirt without the flannel, leaving his arms bare for her perusal. Holy hsit, he was mouth-wateringly sexy without even trying. She watched his hand holding the tattoo gun lift, noticing he wore a ring on his thumb and one on his pointer finger of his right hand. She wondered where he'd gotten them. "I'm a little early," she said, hating the way her voice cracked.

"Have a seat. I'm almost done here." Tymber nodded toward the man on his table.

True to his words, Tymber finished up, walking his client through the care instructions. While he cleaned up, she took in the inside of Twisted Ink. The art lining the walls were gorgeous. She got up to look at one closer.

"Ember painted that. He's an artist with a gun or a brush." Tymber placed his hands on her shoulders, speaking next to her ear. "I won't tell you what else I've heard he's good with."

His warm breath fanning over her flesh sent a shiver of delight through her. "Hmm, well, I'm sure he's all that and a bag of chips. How about you?" she asked, tilting her head to the side.

Tymber dropped a kiss on her exposed neck. "I'm pretty good."

A snort from behind them had her twisting around. The man who spoke had the bluest eyes she'd ever seen, his bad boy grin telling her more than words. "Well, I hope you're better than good," she quipped.

He took a step back, his hand trailing down her arm until he reached her hand. "Come over here and see what I've done."

She let him lead her to his work station where several pieces of paper lay, the quote she'd told him she wanted on each piece, with a slightly different handwriting. "Did you do all these?" she gestured toward the drawings.

"I did two out of the four, Lincoln and Ember did the others. Tell me which you like the best, or if you don't like any, we can start over." As he spoke he tipped his head to where Link was.

Ivy noticed him leaning against the wall, his arms crossed, but she could feel tension crackling in the air. God, what if she chose one he hadn't done? She gave herself a mental shake. This was her body that was being marked forever. Taking the time to study each piece, she kept going back to one in particular. The curling of certain letters made the design seem more...feminine. "This one," she said pointing at the design she could already see on her rib cage.

A bright smile broke across Tymber's face. "Perfect, that one is mine. So, where we inking you?"

Ivy unzipped her jacket, exposing what she wore beneath. "Right here," she indicated her ribs.

"Damn, girl, that's a sensitive place. You sure you want it there?"

Her eyes jumped upward, looking for the speaker. A gorgeous woman with long black hair parted to the side, showing the shaved half of her head strolled in from the back. Her tattoos were colorful, like the woman. "Oh, I want it there alright." Her pain threshold was high, but even so, she was prepared for the feel of the needle.

The woman brought over some papers for her to fill out, making Tymber mutter under his breath.

"I have a set here for her, Lux." He pointed toward the papers lying on the desk.

"Yeah, but sometimes you forget. Did you happen to get one of these signed by your customer last night?" One dark, perfectly shaped brow winged up, challenging Tymber.

He raised his right hand, using his left he began making a rolling motion until his middle finger was extended. "Special circumstances, and for your info, he's filled out the forms before."

Ivy felt like she was watching a tennis match. "Do you two need a moment?" she questioned. The last thing she planned to do was become the middle to another love story, making it a triangle. Nope, she was done with that shit.

"Nah, Lux just thinks she's the boss around here," he teased, winking at Ivy. "Come on, let's put this on you and see if you like the size and placement."

The beautifully written words looked perfect after he peeled back the paper, leaving the outline on her side, just below her breasts and down to her hips. Her black sports bra served as a shirt under the jacket she'd had on, and even now lying on the table, she didn't feel the slightest bit out of her comfort zone. The soft hum of the needle soothed her jagged soul, allowing her to float away while Tymber carefully worked on her tattoo. What seemed like only minutes later, she heard Tymber announce he was done. Her lids lifted. "I fell asleep," she laughed.

"Yep, and you snore. I think Ember is jealous. Wanna see? I added some color around the feather of the pen, and a few more splotches, making it look like a watercolor like you'd described."

She turned until she was sitting, getting her bearing under her. Once she was sure her legs would hold her, she hopped down and walked to the full length mirror. She lifted her arm so she could see the entire piece. "Holy shit, it's gorgeous," she said, not bothering to tamp down the awe she felt.

Tymber stood behind her, his hands still covered by black latex gloves. "I'm glad you like it. Who did the fairy on your back?"

Her shoulders lifted and fell while she kept her eyes pinned to his through the mirror. "One year down in Sturgis I got the bright idea to get a tattoo. The guys vetted the shop for me. I told him what I wanted, and he did a quick sketch, making the fairy appear like I wanted."

Tymber traced her back, his fingers tickling her as if they were electric. "He was good."

She nodded. "I think he was too scared not to…" She shut her mouth, not wanting to taint his relationship with the MC.

"I took the colors from it and incorporated it into this piece, figuring you'd like it." Tymber became no nonsense, covering her with a gel, then a clear plastic was placed over it, secured by tape.

"We still on for dinner?" Ivy didn't look at him while she asked, picking up her purse, digging her wallet out.

Tymber's hand covered hers. "This one's on me."

She snorted. "Actually, it's on me." She tilted her chin down toward her side.

"Cute," he rumbled. "Let's get going, my stomach is eating my backbone."

"Go on, we'll give him shit when he comes back." Lincoln winked, his hand pointed at her. "Don't keep him out too late, though. He's a grump when he doesn't get his eight hours of beauty sleep a night."

Tymber lifted is hand, flipping Lincoln off. "Man, one day you're gonna bite off more than you can chew. I can't wait to see the day you piss someone off who's not your friend."

Lincoln only laughed while another man, an artist she hadn't spoken to, stood up. Her eyes followed his progress, going up and up until she was sure she wasn't seeing correctly. The man had to be like six seven at least.

Her mouth hung open, but she shut it as Tymber tapped her chin. "That's Ember. We're not sure if he's human or an alien from another planet." Tymber motioned toward the giant.

"It's true, girl. Every time I hear of a UFO sighting I ask him if that's his people coming to get him." Lincoln dodged the balled up roll of paper towels aimed at his head. "Dude, careful while I'm working." Lincoln chuckled as the guy laying on his table grunted what she thought was an expletive. "Almost done, how you doing?"

Ivy tried not to laugh, but poor Ember made it hard as he flipped his non-existent hair behind his shoulder. "You boys are just jealous because all your ladies see me and forget about you. Ain't that right, sexy?" he asked, his deep baritone voice filled with laughter, making her smile.

"I'm gonna have to ask you to no." Ivy flicked her hand as if she was shooing him away.

"Excuse me? Ask me to no? What the hell does that mean?" Ember placed his hands on hips that had probably done lots of moving in and out of his lovers' thighs. She was not going to be added to that list.

"It means she thinks you're a dumbass, and has no plans to sleep with you," Lux spoke up from her perch at the receptionist station.

"Let's go before mayhem strikes," Tymber announced.

"Don't you need to—never mind," Ivy stared at his workstation, shocked to see it had been cleaned already.

"You were in the zone, so I picked up before waking you." Tymber shrugged.

Ember cleared his throat. "Seriously, you should maybe check your other prospects before settling on that one. Me for instance, I don't have family issues that'll take me away from whatever we have going on. That one," he stopped and pointed at Tymber. "He's got all kinds of baggage." His smile was pure sin, making Ivy roll her eyes.

"We all have baggage. It's knowing when to toss the trash out that separates us from idiots." She winked at him, waiting to see his reaction.

Ember saluted her with a two finger movement from his brow to his lips. "Well, from one idiot to another, I bid you both a goodnight. I've got a date with a woman who loves how I work."

Tymber tugged her behind him, heading toward the back of the shop. "Wait, my car's out front."

"I thought I'd take us on my bike. There's an overlook that's near the restaurant that's pretty amazing." He halted with his hand on the door leading outside.

His body was loose, letting her know it was her decision. "I don't have a helmet." Why she said that, she didn't know, but damn, she actually wanted to ride behind him.

"I've got one. And before you say anything, I keep one for when my nieces want a ride." He pointed toward the wall where one was hanging next to a couple others. "Come on, take a walk on the wild side," he murmured.

If only he knew just how wild she'd been. However, that was in the past. She wasn't going to pass up a chance to be close to Tymber. Hell, he would probably forget all about her if he knew exactly what her involvement with the MC had been. A wild side he said. The man would rethink his words if he'd ever stepped foot inside the clubhouse. Wild didn't even begin to describe what went down at a party with the MC.

"Alright, but just to warn you, I will squeeze the life out of you if you do anything dangerous," she warned.

Tymber chuckled, making her acutely aware that she hadn't zipped the jacket over her bra, showing off the fact her nipples were hard.

Chapter Five

Tymber tried to keep his gaze from dropping to the hardened nipples pressing against the thin black material, but it was a losing battle. For one, she was one of the sexiest women he'd ever seen. For two, he had his ink on her. All he thought about while he'd been inking her was how fucking sexy she looked, her head pillowed on her jacket while she slept. "You can squeeze me as tightly as you want." And if that was a double entendre, so be it.

Her sigh lifted her breasts up, drawing his attention again.

"I have a feeling anything with you could get twisted into something dirty," she muttered, but smiled.

They walked outside, the night still warm and filled with possibilities. He slung his leg over the bike, strapping the skull cap on once he settled. "It's an art, one I'm a master at."

Ivy put the helmet on, showing she'd done it before. He wondered who, what, where and when, but bit his cheek to keep from asking. One day, he hoped to know all her secrets.

Ivy straddled the bike, her arms coming around him naturally. "Come on then, show me what you can do."

The feel of her tiny body snuggling up to his back, the sweet press of her breasts against him, made him aware he was treading on dangerous grounds. One where his heart was laid open. "I'll keep you safe. Just hold on tight and don't let go." The words meaning more than he let on.

Three weeks later…

Tymber closed up the shop, his hand reaching for his phone on autopilot. The bells above the door rang, making him glance up to find two members of the bikers' club standing in his doorway. "Hey, guys, sorry but we're closed."

"Yeah, who's gonna make us leave?" The two men stood side-by-side, their arms crossed over their chest.

He held his hands up, not realizing he'd already dialed Ivy's number. "Are you wanting a tattoo, or what? If it's cash, well, I'm afraid to say there's probably less than a hundred in the register since most of our clients pay with cards."

No way in hell would he show their appearance shook him.

"You're wanted at the clubhouse. You can either follow us on your own bike, or…" the rest of his sentence was left off.

Tymber eyed the two men. He was sure he could take them both but fucking up the tattoo shop wasn't on his list of things to do this year, or next. "What's this about?" he questioned.

"King will tell you when you get there. You coming on your own, or what?"

Tymber shrugged. "I'll follow you. Although I don't understand what the fuck's going on, I much prefer to arrive on my own than whatever you had planned."

The one who'd done all the talking shoulder bumped the other. "Get his phone. King said he didn't want the cops involved. This wannabe looks like he might try calling the poe poe. Ain't that right, tree?"

At the other man's jibe, Tymber held his phone out, the screen lighting up with Ivy's name. He quickly pressed the side, locking his phone so the two men couldn't go through it. Not that he had anything to hide, but he'd be damned if he allowed them access to his shit.

By the time he pulled into the gravel lot behind the other two bikes, he was seething. He thought of grabbing the gun he kept in his saddle bag but decided against it. Going into the Royal Sons' house with a gun was a sure way to get his ass hurt, shot, or killed.

With ease, he kicked the stand down on his bike, the motorcycle's rumble stopped as soon as he pushed the button, silencing his ride while the other two did the same. The loud thump of music could be heard from inside the spacious looking building. He didn't realize the MC had a home as close to his until they'd began riding up and away from town.

When they'd pulled into a drive that was almost unnoticeable, he began to worry. Lights up ahead had kept him on the path. They passed a home twice the size of his and another smaller yet still big one, before coming to the huge clearing where another building sat, the lights and sounds inside reminiscent of a bar. Only the line of bikes outside, along with a few other vehicles let him know this was where the club met and hung out.

Knowing it would do him no good to ask the two jackasses who'd ridden out with him what was up, he walked forward, waiting at the door for one of them to open it. One didn't just barge into a clubhouse without permission, that he knew from talking to King.

The door opened, the music blaring interrupted his thoughts. "You three gonna stand out here all night or you coming in?"

Tymber looked the other man in the eye, uncaring what protocol suggested. This wasn't the president or the vice president, but his rockers were slightly different than the two other men. Fuck, he swore. They'd sent prospects to get him. Meaning he was screwed. Only he didn't know what he'd done. The last time he'd saw any of the members had been when King came for his last tattoo. That had been almost a month ago, and in the weeks between, he'd done nothing but work and spend time with Ivy. Damn, he wondered if she was pissed at him for standing her up. Tonight, he'd planned to cook her dinner at his place. He didn't have any plans past that, other than to go with the flow. Hell, for weeks he'd gone to bed with her name on his lips, her taste in his mouth, yet he still hadn't pushed their relationship to the next level. Not because his body didn't ache to fill hers, but for the first time, he wanted to get to know the woman, wanted to build something that was more than sex. Finally, he was sure they had that, with the promise of more. Yet, here he was, being led into the lions' den like a sheep to the slaughterhouse.

"Ah, I'm glad you could make it. Did my prospects give you any shit?"

Tymber barely kept from jumping at the words spoken so close to his ear. He hadn't even seen the man come up, let alone felt the air stir as he moved into his space. "They were very closed lipped on why I was being summoned up here. No, I take that back. They mentioned something about me not liking it if they had to force me. So here I am, what the fuck's going on?" He turned, leveling King with his stare.

King slapped him on the shoulder, then steered them toward the back. People parted for them without being told, giving Tymber an idea of the power this man had. He almost wished he could call back the challenging words.

"I always did like you, Tymber. First time I met you, I knew you had grit." King swept his arm out in front of him. "You hungry, thirsty?"

Women lay on the long tables, their bodies on display with different assortment of food placed strategically on them. He shook his head at the offer. The only body he wanted to eat off of was Ivy's.

"Drink? You know it's rude not to accept an offer from your host?" King snagged a bottle of beer from one of the buckets on the table between the two women. He then ran the cold bottle up the calf and inner thigh of the one on the left. The redhead closed her eyes, moaning at his actions.

Tymber didn't want the bottle that had just been rubbed all over the woman. His hand reached for a bottle, glad when nobody struck out at him. "Thanks," Tymber said after he downed half the contents of the cold brew.

"My pleasure. Now, let's have a seat and talk, shall we?" King made another sweeping motion, getting people to move from their spots, leaving two chairs open plus the one at the head which clearly belonged to the president.

Tymber sat in one of the chairs, the fine hair on the nape of his neck standing on end. "While I appreciate the hospitality, why don't you tell me exactly what's brought me here?" He took another healthy swig from the bottle.

King tipped his bottle toward IIIIII. "You know, I always liked you. You do good work and don't seem to shake easily. I admire that in a man. Now, I got a question for you, and I want you to think before you answer."

Placing the bottle on the table, he waited for King to continue. Fuck, he swore the entire place had gone quiet, yet he could still hear music. "I'm always honest. No reason not to be. Besides, it cuts the bullshit down when you just spit shit out truthfully."

"You fucking Ivy, and if so for how long? And, before you think to get stupid, know your answers are very important to your health." King's hand flexed and unflexed on the table.

Shit. Was she one of theirs? He tried to think back to the past few weeks. There'd been no sign of a boyfriend nor did she let on she knew the club when he'd talked about tattooing King that first night. "My first inclination is to tell you it's none of your business, but I have a feeling that's not going to go down really well."

King nodded. "You'd be right. So, what's your answers? Do I need to ask the questions again or are you just working up the courage to tell me to my face you been fucking my brother's old lady?"

Shock held him immobile for a second. "What the fuck do you mean? Your brothers' old lady?"

King motioned to someone behind him, but Tymber kept his eyes on the leader, his next words would be a defining moment in his life.

"Ivy is my brother Luke's girl, didn't you know?"

"I'm not nor have I ever been any of the club members' old lady," Ivy shouted.

Tymber jumped up, reaching out for Ivy, only to come up short as another member shoved the tip of a knife near his throat. "The Prez ain't done talking to you," the guttural words said with such menace, silenced him.

"Rooster, back the fuck off him with that knife, or so help me I'll be shoving it so far up your ass the sun will be the last thing you think about," Ivy warned. Her heart had been racing the entire drive from outside Twisted Ink and didn't seem ready to slow a bit.

"Everyone out," King said, his voice booming above the other sounds.

It wasn't a hot night, but she swore her entire body had to be sweating from fear and adrenalin. She kept her eyes on Rooster and his wicked looking knife. The man was a lover of making his point with a blade. She shifted her focus to King, moving forward, her hand brushing Tymber's. "I'm sorry," she whispered.

"Alright, now that the only ones here are family." King nodded, waiting until the entire MC club seemed to surround them.

Ivy thought they'd be somewhat safe since there were others around who weren't fully patched members who'd brought their old ladies. She should have known King didn't play by one set of rules. "King, it's me you're mad at. Let Tymber go and I'll—" she licked her lips before continuing in a firm tone. "I'll do whatever you ask of me, just don't fuck with him."

King gave a dry chuckle, sitting back down in his chair as if he didn't have a care in the world. Tymber's arms flexed, showing the muscles and strength he had within him. She didn't doubt one bit he could take on any member of the Royal MC and probably win. However, he'd be taking on more than just one man.

"Sit, Ivy. We've things to discuss." King tapped the table, expecting obedience.

"Look, King, I don't know what the fuck is going on, but this shit ain't cool," Tymber growled.

Ivy turned to see what Rooster did to Tymber. There were rules in an MC. One of them being respect the President. Tymber's little outburst could be deemed disrespectful. Her focus was ensnared by the man who she cared too much about. Within the club, the golden rule is that club comes first, loyalty and commitment to the wellbeing of the club is always first priority. This is never to be questioned. After club then comes the brothers and sisters, family, friends, job, personal possessions and even personal safety.

"Ah, look at that, boys, she's already replaced my brother," King said. His voice that deadly quiet.

She'd only heard him use that tone when he was pissed or discussing club business. The fact he was allowing Tymber to stay while she and he had their talk wasn't good. Nobody but club members were allowed when discussing anything club related.

"You know there's two types of people in the world in my mind. There's my brothers and sisters, and then there's those who are a potential threat to our club. Which do you think your friend falls into, Ivy?" King let the silence linger, then he pointed to the chair again. "I suggest you sit down, little girl, unless you want to see my bad side come out."

It took her seconds to do as he said, her heart pounded in her chest with fear and anger she was having to go through this. "Why?" she asked.

King sat back, his arms crossing over his chest, drawing her gaze to the cut he wore and the patch that marked him as President. "Let's start by discussing why you've not answered my calls or texts for the past couple months."

She tried to keep her hands from shaking as she placed them on the table. "I...I didn't know what to say. I think you said it all at—" she swallowed the lump in her throat. "You said enough the last time we spoke. I figured it would be best if I removed myself from, everything."

"When we took you in, I promised Luke I'd look out for you. You promised to look out for Luke. Seems we're not keeping up to our promises. Want to tell me why?"

"Dammit, what do you want from me?" she cried.

King sat forward, his face inches from hers. "I want the fucking truth, and I want it now."

God, her throat felt dry, the need for liquid courage made her wish she'd gotten a drink before interrupting what was happening. Of course, she probably would've thrown it up the way her stomach was cramping. "I met Tymber only a few weeks ago. He's not part of this."

King got in her face, the scent of beer and mint wafted to her as he spoke. "He's a part of this as long as I say he is. Ain't that right, Rooster?"

His words had her swinging her head around. "That's right. Want me to make him less pretty?" Rooster asked.

"For fucksake, what did you expect me to do? I didn't go out looking for a man. Nobody can replace Luke," she swore.

"In that you're correct. Let me tell you a story, shall we?" he continued without waiting for her to respond. "You and my baby brother have been together since before either of you had grown any pubic hair. Now, my brother's dead because you decided you wanted that pretty boy, Darian. My brother couldn't handle your cheating on him, so he took the cowards way out." The last was said in a near yell.

"That's not true. King, you have to believe me. Luke was my best friend, my only true friend in the world. I'd never hurt him like that." She stayed where she was, her face mere inches from a fuming King.

"I know that, dammit. Now, why don't you tell me what my brother was too chicken shit to do, and we'll go from there."

Her eyes darted around the gathered members, hating the thought of anyone but King and Duke, Luke's brothers to hear. However, it appeared as though Tymber's life was on the line. "King, please, tell everyone to clear out first," she begged, her voice a small whisper.

"These are our family, Ivy. You are family. Whatever you gotta say, just say it." King's hand smacked the table, making her jump back in the seat.

She looked to Duke, hoping he'd step forward, and do what, she didn't know, but if there was anything he could do, she wanted him to do it. "Duke, this is your twin brother's personal business."

will be sporting a new scar."

She heard Tymber grunt seconds after the sound of what had to be another member hitting him. "Fine, you want to know, I'll tell you. However, you need to know this isn't something I say lightly. I promised Luke to never..." she broke off, a sob escaping her trembling lips.

Commotion behind her made her look away from King's penetrating gaze. The breath froze in her throat while she watched Tymber grab Rooster's wrist, twisting and turning until he was the one behind the brother, the deadly looking knife placed against Rooster's throat. "I don't fucking like to be choked, feel me?" He gave Rooster a little shake, keeping the knife steady without cutting the throat he had it pressed against.

"Tymber, what're you gonna do, fight all of us?" King asked.

Tymber shrugged. "If I gotta, yeah. I've faced bigger shit than this." He gave Rooster a shove.

"Wait. Just stop everyone. King, you have the power to stop all of this." She half stood from her seat, halting at King's glare.

"I didn't have the power to protect my baby brother. Let's cut the shit, and you speak," he growled, stabbing his finger toward Ivy.

She licked her lips, her focus bouncing from King to Tymber. "Won't you let him leave first. This is club business, and he's not…"

"I know what he is and what he ain't, little girl." King placed his hand over hers, stopping the nervous twitch.

"I'm sorry, Tymber. I didn't mean to bring you into this…mess. King, can I ask you a question?" At his nod, she inhaled deeply, the familiar scent of booze, sex, and smoke filling her lungs. "Would you love your brother no matter what?"

"Just spill it out, or so help me, I'm not going to be responsible for what happens."

A grunt followed by cursing had her tensing, attempting to stand again, only to be pushed back down by Traeger. She glared at the big bastard, then finally, realizing there was no getting around her telling King what he wanted. "Darian wasn't my boyfriend, King. He was Luke's. I loved Luke, and he loved me, but it was a brother and sister love."

Silence greeted her announcement.

Chapter Six

Tymber didn't want to hurt a member of the Royal Sons, but he'd be damned if he allowed one hair on Ivy's head to be hurt. It was a lesson in control he was sure he didn't have, to allow Rooster with his big ass knife to hold him. His control snapping as the man decided to wrap his big beefy arms around his neck. Tymber was many things, but a fool or pussy wasn't one of them. If the Royals wanted a fight, he'd give 'em one.

"If one more fucker tries to sneak up on me, I promise I won't play nice," he warned.

King's warning completely ignored as he twisted at the last second, missing the punch aimed at his head. He grabbed the bastard who tried to sucker punch him by the arm, flipping him over his back so that he landed in front of him, a look of shock on the younger man's face. The knife he'd taken from Rooster was big, but he avoided cutting the fucker, barely.

"Settle," King uttered the one word.

Tymber stepped around the sprawled man, walked up to the one named Rooster, keeping his focus on what was going on around him. He flipped the knife around, handing the blade back by the handle. "I meant no disrespect, but having shit like that shoved in my face, brings back memories I'd rather not have."

"Ivy, you telling me my brother never stuck his dick in you?"

He wanted to punch King in the mouth for the way his question made Ivy jump. "What's it matter now? I'm sorry your brother died, but what the hell does Ivy have to do with it?"

"My brother killed himself because he caught her with another son-of-a-bitch. Ain't that right, Ivy?" Duke, the quieter of the brothers spoke up. Menace and anger filling his features, twisting what was probably a good looking guy, into something ugly.

Ivy was shaking her head, her hands still trapped under King's. "No, that's not what happened. Your brother...Luke thought you knew about him and Darian. He said you caught them together?"

King jerked back like he'd been struck. "Are you telling me it was my fault he offed himself?"

This time it was Tymber who jerked, looking toward Ivy for confirmation. He'd first seen her outside the suicide meeting and had thought it was her who was contemplating killing herself. He ran a tired hand down his face, sighing loudly. "King, its nobody's fault for Luke's choice to end his life. Fuck, I should know. If I had gone through with my dark thoughts, I could've done the same thing. I had to pull myself out of depression and decide that living was better than being six feet under. I did that. I would've been the one to end my life, same as your brother."

Ivy's whispered, *no* was the only word uttered for minutes.

"Everyone out except Duke," King ordered.

Traeger, the Sergeant of Arms grunted. "Do you think that's wise?" he questioned.

"I ain't scared she's gonna slit my throat or afraid of that one leaping across this table. I got this." King stood up as he spoke, each word coming out from between gritted teeth.

Tymber stayed where he was, listening as Ivy told them about her and Luke's bargain. From where he stood, she didn't gain shit, except a bullseye on her chest.

"You look ready to spit nails. Fuck, my brother was gay and was scared to tell me." King shook his head, his hands scrubbed down his face.

"He was scared you'd kick him out of the club. I tried to tell him you wouldn't, but he wasn't prepared to listen. I don't know what you saw with him and Darian, but it was enough to make him think you knew. Combine that with his depression, he felt he had no option. I…I have a letter from him to you. Don't do that." She stopped speaking as King ground his teeth loud enough he could hear it as well.

"Where's this fucking note, Ivy?" King squeezed her hand, pain reflecting on her face.

"Get your fucking hands off of her or so help me God, I won't be responsible for my actions."

Tymber took the few steps separating him from Ivy. "Baby, do you have the letter?" he asked in a soft tone.

Ivy nodded, looking toward the floor where her bag had fallen. King walked around the table, bent, and then dumped her purse's contents onto the smooth surface in front of her. Her hands fumbled for the letter, sifting through a few pieces of mail she'd had in it before pulling it out. "It's right here. I didn't read it, though."

The charged atmosphere heightened as King read the note with Duke looking over his shoulder, both men freezing for a few minutes, their shoulders lifted and fell. King balled the paper up. "Motherfucker," he roared, his fist slamming into the table, making the bottles on top fall off, shattering glass echoed around them.

"Why have you skipped out on us if you weren't guilty? Why'd I have to virtually kidnap a man to get you here?" King asked, moving around to take his seat back.

"After you had a couple members break into our apartment and beat the shit out of Darian, I felt it was in my best interest to make myself scarce. I'd planned...I mean, I thought about leaving, but..." she trailed off.

Tymber stared at Ivy, then King. "You were at the center because you were thinking of killing yourself, weren't you?" The knowledge had his gut rolling.

She shrugged. "I didn't have anything to lose or to live for. My family has always been Luke and his family. Without them, I had nothing."

He didn't care about protocol anymore. His arms moved with no fear of consequences, pulling Ivy into his embrace. "You have so much to live for, Ivy. You hear me?" He gave her a shake, wanting her to acknowledge his words.

"I thought he was bi, not gay," Duke muttered. His head in his hands as he spoke. Bent over in the chair, he looked gutted. "He was my twin. How did

I not know what he was going through?" Duke stood, the chair scraping loudly behind him, falling on its side in a crash. "Who'd you have go rough up their place?" he asked King.

King held his hands up. "I didn't."

"Yes, you did. Darian said the guys had on their cuts and told him he was gonna pay for Luke's—his death."

"Either Darian," King spat the name out. "is lying or someone took it upon themselves. You know who I believe, don't you?"

She reached for her phone lying in the middle of the table. "Darian saved them coming and going on our security camera. I didn't look, but I know he wasn't lying. My door didn't just get broke down on its own, King."

King grabbed the phone with the glitter shit of a cover on it. "Show me," he ordered.

He almost felt bad for the fear and anxiety he could see stamped on Ivy's little face. Almost being the key word. Once she put her code in, she handed him the phone. He opened the app for the security company, his thumb hovering over the key that said *Event History*. One push and the dates began to pop up. He scrolled down, stabbing at the date in question. "Fuck," he muttered as he watched two prospects enter the building. The next saved event was over an hour later. Again, he hit the button, watching Frog and Groot swagger out. From the looks of the two men, they were proud of whatever they'd done. "Duke, get Frog and Groot in here."

He barely controlled the urge to bust the phone held in his palm, anger surging through him like lava. If he wanted to see his brother alive again, he knew all he had to do was scroll back a couple more weeks and see if there were any saved events. Instead of following through on the impulse, he sat the phone down, the last video still displayed.

"Have a seat, fuckers," Duke growled.

Ivy looked toward the two men, her hate clear as the green in her eyes. King knew then if she'd have had a gun, she'd have shot the two bastards.

He wasn't far behind in his thoughts. "You need to tell me anything?" King asked, breaking into the silence.

It took the two idiots less than two minutes to turn on each other, each blaming the other for their actions. "We were going to tell you, but then we noticed some things," Frog muttered.

"Well, don't stop now." King waved him on.

He listened to the men explain how they'd began trashing the place after beating the shit out of the man who'd been there. "So, you decided to fuck up my brother's home without asking me for permission?"

Again, each of them spoke over the other until he had enough. "Groot, shut the fuck up. Frog, what made you decide your actions? Let me warn you, if I don't like what you say, there's going to be consequences."

Frog's words brought his mind to a hard stop. "You didn't share a bedroom with Luke?"

Ivy shook her head, tears leaking down her cheeks.

"This Darian, he was important to Luke?" King asked, his hand balling into a fist. Control, he needed to get his shit back under control. Ivy's dark head nodding up and down pissed him off. "Why did he hide from me what was essentially his life?" he breathed out loudly.

"He loved you both, worshipped you. He just...he was scared." Ivy lifted her hand, placing it on top of his.

"Tymber, sorry you got pulled in the way you did. I know how stubborn this one is, and one of my guys said he'd seen you two together on several occasions. I took a chance and, well shit, here we are."

King could see the war raging in Tymber's eyes. On one hand, he knew the bastard wanted to punch him, yet he also didn't want to show too much disrespect. He put his other hand over Ivy's. "You two get out of here. I've some things to take care of, but Ivy," he said, waiting until she met his stare. "You're still family. You'll always be family."

Ivy's chin wobbled, more tears flowed from her eyes. "Thanks, King."

He sat back, waving his hand, he dismissed her and Tymber. However, the man didn't seem to be mollified. "You got something to say?" King raised one brow.

Tymber leaned down, so he was on the same level as King. "What happened tonight wasn't cool, but I know you were doing what you felt was right. Next time you want a meet and greet with me, call first. I don't like having my chain jerked even by someone I liked and respected."

"That sounds past tense, Tymber. I suppose I owe you an apology?"

He grinned as time ticked by. Frog and Groot shuffled their boots in the ensuing silence.

"Was that your apology?" Tymber asked, pulling Ivy into his side.

"That's as good as you're gonna get. Now get the fuck outta here. Ivy, don't be a stranger, girl."

When the two walked out, he speared his prospects with a glare. "Now, let's have a talk, boys, shall we?"

Tymber walked out with Ivy under his arm. He was shocked to see so many standing around, waiting outside for whatever they were anticipating happening. He'd be damned if it was a show of him getting his ass kicked.

"I suggest you stand the fuck down," Tymber warned.

"Let them through, King's orders." Traeger moved away from the crowd, coming into the circle they'd formed around Tymber and Ivy, speaking loudly enough he could be heard over the murmurs.

"I'll follow you, Ivy." Tymber didn't take his eyes off of Traeger.

His breath stalled in his throat as she did what he said. He then proceeded to where he'd parked his bike, happy to see they hadn't fucked it up. "Thanks for the hospitality." Tymber fired his motorcycle up, using his feet he moved it backward. The red lights from Ivy's Bronco flashed, showing Tymber she was stopping. He lifted two fingers, saluting Traeger before he followed Ivy. Fuck, his damn heart was near to bursting. Usually he'd go for a long ride and get his head on straight. Instead, he followed Ivy as they rode out of the driveaway. A mile or so down the road, her Bronco swerved to the right, coming to a jarring stop on one of the scenic lookouts that dotted the highway. He let his bike come to a rolling stop next to her rig, waiting until she glanced his way. In his hurry to follow he hadn't put his helmet on, which normally would've been his first move. Now, he set the stand down after turning the key, The cool night air ruffled his hair while he sat, waiting for her to look his way.

When her head turned, and those eyes that were so green he swore he could get lost in them met his, he knew then and there he'd fallen in love for the first time. He dismounted the bike with ease, moving toward her. The driver's door flung open, and then he found himself holding onto a sobbing Ivy.

"You fool," she whispered.

Tymber palmed the back of her head. "Is that all you're gonna say?"

Ivy stood on her toes, her body shaking, not from cold, but the release of tension he was sure. "They could've killed you."

Gripping a handful of her hair in his fist, he made sure she couldn't look away. "You shouldn't have followed us."

Ivy slapped his chest once, twice, three times, then her hands went around his neck, pulling him down to her. "I will always follow you."

He looked around them, the dark night lit by stars and the soft glow of the moon the only lights. In the still of the moment, he bent, taking her lips in a kiss that was a claiming. She was his, and he'd make damn sure nobody else could hurt her.

The need for oxygen had him breaking away from her lips, her arms around his neck squeezed. "We need to go before my body overtakes my mind and I end up fucking you where we stand," he muttered, kissing her again because he could do nothing else.

"I don't care where we are. I want you now." She released her hold, wriggling until he dropped his arms. Staring transfixed at the sight before him, he swore he was in heaven as her top was pulled over her head, then tossed aside. Her eyes held him spellbound while her fingers unsnapped her bra, giving him a glimpse of the perfect mounds while she peeled one side back then the other, her shoulders rolling helped her remove the scraps of silk and lace.

"Fuck, you're gonna kill me." In all honesty, he'd die happily if he was buried inside Ivy.

She unsnapped the button on her jeans, the sound of her zipper going down excited the fuck out of him. For too many nights he'd fantasized about seeing all of her laid out before him. Again, he looked around the clearing. "Wait," he ordered, stopping the shimming she was doing to get the tight as fuck denim off. He scooped her off the ground and carried her around to the passenger side, opening the door with one hand while still holding her with the other. Slowly, he let her slide down his front, the sweet sensation of her hard little nipples scraped against his shirt covered chest. He had yet to show her his scars from the removal of the cancer and the surrounding tissue. Hell, he wasn't sure if he'd ever told her the extent of his fight. A fight he won and was at the five year mark, meaning he was considered cancer free. Not in remission, but in the clear.

"There's something I need you to know," he broke eye contact, looking over the city below.

"Whatever it is, if you're not married or have a girlfriend, and you're not gay, which I'd be fine with, but clearly we'd have to—"

Tymber silenced her ramblings with a kiss, his body aching to feel her nakedness against him. "Lets get a few things straight. One, I'm not now nor have I ever been attracted to men. Two, I don't have a woman in my life, other than my sisters and nieces. Three, I'm done talking for the moment, woman. Take those jeans off unless you don't like them, which I'd then happily destroy as I stripped you. Your decision." He waited, watching Ivy's chest move up and down was a work of art.

"What about you?" Her sassy words were accompanied by a grin.

He undid the top button on his jeans, the crown of his dick sprung free from the tight confines. "I don't want to get caught with my clothes off, but I promise you this, once I get you to my place, you can explore 'til your heart's content."

Her hand moved, the tip of her finger ran over the top, spreading the moisture over the head. "What about me?"

"Trust me, if anyone shows up, I'll be able to keep them occupied until you're dressed. I have a feeling I won't be wanting anyone else to see this body but me," he groaned at the feel of her hand fisting his dick. "Pants off, Ivy," he ordered.

He sighed at the loss of her touch, until seeing her shimmy the jeans down her legs, taking a little scrap of lace with them. She stood straight, letting him look at her. "Fuck you're perfect."

With her jeans below her, she knelt, grabbed his jeans and opened the fly further. Tymber nearly came at the sight of her kneeling before him, her pink little tongue swiping over her lips. God, he wanted to feel her mouth on him. "You planning on staring at my dick all night?"

Ivy leaned in, placing a kiss to the top of his aching cock, then swiped her tongue across, moaning as she slipped her mouth over the end. Tymber tunneled his hand into her hair, palming the back of her head, guiding her in the rhythm he wanted. She kept one hand on the base, keeping him from going too far. Pulling off, she looked up at him. "I can't take it all," she explained.

He nodded, giving her head a little tug. "Babe, what you're doing is perfect."

Ivy licked the tip again, her eyes fluttering closed. Tymber wanted to order her to look at him, but he too felt the need to close his eyes and enjoy. Only the image of her, on her knees sucking him was one he didn't want to miss. He let her suck him for a few more minutes, each second was a lesson in control. Finally, he tugged her off him, lifting her to a standing position. "The first time I come with you, I want it inside your pussy, not your mouth. Although I do reserve the right to replay this scenario again."

"But I was enjoying myself," Ivy pouted.

He placed her on the leather seat of her passenger side, his body moving between her thighs. "So was I, baby." He stared down at her gorgeous body, spread out like an offering across the front seat of her vehicle. "Damn, I could look at you for days and still not have my fill of you."

Ivy trailed her hand down her chest, tweaking both pert nipples before moving down to cover her mound. "I need you now," she breathed out.

Wanting to give her what she wanted and what he needed, he moved back a pace, then he did what he wanted, taking her left breast into his mouth, sucking the tip before releasing it and doing the same to its twin. Ivy ground against him, his dick so fucking hard he was sure he'd come two seconds after entering her. He gave her nibbling kisses, sucking the skin between his lips, leaving his mark on her until he reached paradise at the apex of her thighs. "I love this," he whispered, running his nose through the neatly trimmed hair at the top. He spread her lips open, closing his lips over the hardened bundle of nerves. With his thumbs holding her open, he licked her from top to bottom, making her moan. He shifted, using one hand to spread those sweet pink lips, exposing her to his gaze, to his taking. "You're beautiful." He slipped a finger inside, the warm wetness meeting him let him know she was on board and enjoying what he was doing. Adding a second finger, he pumped them in slowly while he licked her clit in a circular motion.

The flex and release on his fingers came seconds before she moaned his name. He pumped in and out with both fingers, making sure to let her ride out her orgasm. Once he was sure she was finished, he fished into the back pocket of his jeans, taking out his wallet, he pulled a condom out.

She stared at him, then sat up. "Let me." Ivy took the small foil wrapper, opening it with her teeth. In what he swore was an act to kill a man, she rolled the latex over his swollen dick.

He couldn't contain the thrust of his hips at her ministrations. "Damn, you done playing yet?" he questioned, running his finger through her folds. He used her wetness to coat his cock, hating the need for the condom.

"I was done playing a long time ago, Tymber." Ivy placed one foot on the dash, the other on the seat of the Bronco. "Please, make love to me."

Tymber shook his head. "You never have to beg me, unless I ask you to, Ivy."

With her hand guiding him, he pressed forward, watching the tip of his dick disappear inside Ivy, a vision he would always remember. In shallow thrusts, he moved in and out, going slowly so he didn't hurt her. He lifted two fingers to her mouth, his dick jerked at the sight of her sucking them like she'd done his dick just moments ago. With a little pop, he brought the now wet tips to her clit, rubbing in slow tight circles, at the same time he began moving faster. In, out, in, slow, fast and then slow again. The flex and tightening surrounding him made it harder to hold back. "I'm close. Come with me, let me feel you coming around my cock, Ivy."

Her hips swiveled, eyes glassy, she gasped for air. "Harder. Fuck me harder."

Tymber pulled almost all the way out, watching her body as he pushed back in, then repeated the motion, slamming back inside harder, rubbing her clit at the same time. The near stranglehold of her inner muscles made it almost impossible for him to hold back, yet he did. "I want to hear you. Tell me what you nccd, baby."

Ivy's mouth opened on a silent scream, moaning as he pulled back. "Dammit, fuck me harder, faster," she gasped.

He looked down to where they were connected, then up at her. A grin tilting his lips as he lifted his fingers off her clit. With a wink, he used his left hand to hold her open, the tiny bundle of flesh exposed to the night air and him, he gave her a little tap with his right hand. The instant flutter around his girth had him moaning. Another tap, this one a bit harder and on top of her clit instead of her mound made her squeal. Close. He was so fucking close, but so was she.

Two quick slaps to her pussy made her scream his name, her pussy clamping down on him like a vice. He swore he saw heaven when his name was yelled out, her hips rolling and opening for his thrusts. With a groan, he let himself go, the tingle at the base of his spine no longer ignored as he came, calling her name.

"Motherfuck, that was amazing," he panted. Leaning down, he kissed her, loving every unique flavor that was Ivy. "Now that we've taken the edge off, think you can drive to my place? It's literally a five mile drive from here."

"I don't know. I'm not sure my body is my own yet." She wrapped her legs around his waist, locking him inside her.

Tymber felt his cock twitch, but pulled out, the condom filled with come. "Come on, I'll make this up to you."

Ivy sat up, their bodies almost touching. "If you plan to do better than that, I think we need to have a doctor on standby."

He had to agree, them coming together was the best thing he'd ever experienced. However, he was ready to try again just as soon as he got her to his place. He helped her to her feet, unable to stop his hands from smoothing over her sweet little ass. "Get dressed, Ivy. I'd tell you to drive naked, but I don't want to push our luck." The thought of someone coming upon her while she was undressed made his inner caveman rear its head.

He picked up her shirt, shaking it off before handing it to her. She slipped her panties on, then slid the top over her head. Her jeans were next, but first he shook them out, not wanting her to get dirty with the dust and gravel that littered the ground where the jeans had been laying. While she shimmied into the black denim, he adjusted his own clothes. "Follow me," he said once he had her sitting in the front seat behind the wheel.

Ivy lifted her hand, her finger curling toward her. "I need a kiss first."

Chapter Seven

Ivy loved the slight scratch from his beard as he rubbed his cheek against hers, after giving her a kiss that nearly stole her breath. Her body still tingled from his possession, but god, she was ready for round two.

She drove behind him as butterflies danced in her stomach. The slow pace this time was different than the one up to the clubhouse. A shiver wracked her as she thought of all the ways the meeting could've gone sideways. Her lips trembled at the image of Rooster holding a knife to his throat. "Never again," she promised the night. The club had been her life before. Now, her life was going to be whatever she made it. She just hoped Tymber wanted to be a part of her life after what he went through. "I'll convince him some way."

A bright star above flared, drawing her attention. She smiled at the sight of a shooting star crossing above her. She kept her eyes open and on the taillight of Tymber's Harley as she made a wish.

Looking back up, the streaking star was gone. "I loved you, Luke," she said in a low tone, letting the night take her words away through the open top of the Bronco. And she had loved Luke just as he'd loved her. If either of them could've changed him, she was sure they'd have done it. Life wasn't all sunshine and roses, She knew that from her time living with her mother and her stepdad. Yeah, she'd had it bad, but some had it worse. With Tymber, she wanted a fresh start, yet she didn't want to forget her past. Every mark, every memory, is what made her who she was today, warts and all.

As promised, Tymber slowed his bike, turning onto a drive that was nearly as hidden as the Royal Sons clubhouse. Her breath caught in her throat at the view in front of her. His home looked like an old farmhouse, combined with an industrial structure. The concrete part wasn't as cold stacked against the barn like structure. Lights lit up the front in a rainbow of colors.

Pulling up next to him, she twisted the key, letting silence greet her. "This is beautiful." Beautiful and expensive.

"This is or rather was my grandparents' place. I was left it when they both passed away." He stood just outside her door, waiting for her to make a move.

Oh, she was aware he wanted her like she wanted him, but he was letting her make the choice. Stay or go. Her door creaked as she shoved it open. "Do I get a tour?"

His chuckle made all her girly parts stand up and sing. "You really want a tour?"

Ivy hopped down, shaking her head. "Later," she said.

Her words triggered his need, making him eliminate the space between them. "Grab whatcha need, baby. This is going to be a long night."

"Shit, my purse and everything is back at the clubhouse."

"We'll worry about that tomorrow. Tonight, it's about you and me." At her nod, he leaned his shoulder into her stomach, lifting her onto him. "Woman, I hope you know I plan to stamp my claim on every delectable inch of you. If you aren't on board with that, tell me no."

Ivy laughed, her hands going into his back pockets, giving a squeeze to each firm cheek. "Oh no, your wallet's gone."

Tymber slapped her ass, then pulled the wallet out of the front pocket of his jeans, a chain connected to the end kept him from misplacing the thing. He punched in the code to his front door, opening it once the locks disengaged. He moved forward, the alarm blinking red told him nobody had been there since he'd left. With a quick motion, he put the numbers into the keypad, waiting until the box blinked green. Once he made sure the door was locked, he set the alarm again. He didn't want to be disturbed by unwanted visitors. Small lights illuminated the hallways, allowing him to see his way to his bedroom, Ivy's silence almost unnerved him.

"You still with me?" he asked.

"You can't get rid of me. I'm like a tick on a hound dogs back," she joked.

At the side of his bed, he laughed. "I'll show you hound dog," he warned, tossing her down onto the huge California King bed. "There's something I want to show you, something I should've explained before."

Ivy scrambled up, sitting on her knees facing him. "Whatever it is, just say it. Surely, it's worse in your mind than reality?"

Tymber touched the lamp next to the bed, the soft glow giving light to the darkened room. "I should've opened the curtains." He motioned toward the bank of windows across from the bed.

"Quit stalling and tell me. I'm assuming the light is so you can see my reactions?" Ivy bit down on her lip.

"I always was better at showing than telling," he muttered. His eyes locked on hers. He grabbed the bottom of the T-shirt, pulling it over his head, the material held in front of him. "I, fuck. I had cancer. Breast. I mean I had breast cancer. I had a partial mastectomy followed by a round of chemo."

Ivy's hand covered her mouth, horror lit her green stare. "Are you, okay?"

He tossed the black T-shirt onto the hamper. "Yeah, I'm at the five year mark." He explained what that meant.

"Your tattoo, did you get it to cover the scars?" She shuffled closer to the edge of the bed.

Tymber turned away, not wanting to see pity on her face. "I already had a tattoo that covered my chest. Once I knew I was going to live, I decided to have plastic surgery to fix the outer package. The meetings helped with the inner package."

"At the center that night. You were at a cancer survivors meeting?"

He looked over his shoulder, floored to see her standing next to his bed taking off her clothes. "What're you doing?" he asked, his body immediately reacting to her nudity.

Ivy walked up to him, her naked body perfection to him. "Did you think I would turn away because of that?"

The curtains concealed them inside, but he wanted out. Or at least able to see out. With a press of a button, the blackout curtains parted, giving them a glimpse of the pool beyond. "In all honesty, I didn't know." He turned fully toward her.

Ivy jumped at the last second, his arms opening for the little spitfire. "Mmm, I wanted to do that since I first laid eyes on you." She wiggled around, her legs locked behind his back, her arms around his neck. "So much better than in my fantasies."

Tymber smiled, unable to stop himself. "You comfy?" The palms of his hands held her ass, the firm globes a perfect fit for him.

She tugged on his hair, almost like he did to her. "Now, where were we? Oh, you thought I was a shallow beotch who couldn't love you because of your scars, or the fact you kicked cancer's ass? Silly man, I'd love you even if you were a roadmap of scars. We all have scars, some are outside like yours, but some are inside, like mine." She pressed her lips over his, keeping whatever he had to say inside. "I've not told you my sordid past, not completely. If you found out I used to be a junkie, or gave a baby up for adoption, would you think less of me?"

His fingers dug into the flesh nestled in his palms. "Fuck no. Did you?"

"No, but I could've. The reason Luke and I were so close, was mainly because we'd known each other since we started school. I told him I'd fallen in love with him, and one day we'd be married. He'd just beat Tommy Smith up for pulling my pigtails and making me cry. As only a boy would do, he snorted and went off to play. Then, in junior high, he told me he loved me and would marry me one day after I punched Sally Belle for breaking his heart. It was only as we hit high school and I kissed him we realized it wasn't how we expected. There wasn't this big explosion of uncontrollable urges from either of us, but we still tried. Hell, I was naked, and he was only in a pair of boxer briefs. When his dick didn't even twitch, we agreed we were better off as friends. Now, I will say, we fooled around, but it just wasn't meant to be. Our junior year, he fell in lust for the first time, and I...that was when I showed up on his doorstep, bleeding."

Tymber tightened his arms around Ivy. "Why were you bleeding?" he gritted out.

"My stepdad decided it was time I earned my keep. I was sixteen, and he...he assumed I'd been screwing Luke so why not him. That night, I lost my birth family only to gain another, this one by choice and acceptance. King is a hardass, but there was nobody I trusted more than him and the club. They made sure my mother and her husband left town after Luke kicked the shit out of him. Heck, probably the entire state, or they'd face King, who was ten times worse than Luke. Trust me, leaving was the better option." Tears fell from her eyes, memories of that time clearly still painful.

"I'm glad you had them, even though I still want to punch him in the mouth," he said only half joking.

"I'm happy you didn't follow through with that tonight. I know many think an MC is nothing but outlaws and men whose sole purpose is to fuck shit up, but that's not the truth. The week following my escape from the fucker and my mom, I realized that wearing a patch was more than getting together for shits and giggles. Sure, there was a lot of that, but the MC was a family that banded together no matter what. Not one man looked at the other and thought 'how can they help me' within the club. When you commit to the lifestyle, you're given a family who look for ways to help each other. They, as a whole, always look to give, never expecting to receive. To many, it may sound idealistic, and yeah, I think there's probably clubs like that, but not the Royal Sons. Not King and his brothers. I literally had the clothes on my back when I became one of them. No, women aren't patched members, but I was still a Royal. I never had to worry if someone would be there to catch me when I fell. They may be psychotic, a little twisted, and a whole lot fucked up, but they're family. Blood or not, we're a hodgepodge of individuals banding together, blending as one big fucked up family, but that's what they were and would always be, family. Royally twisted was what Luke and I called us."

Tymber let her cry, holding her in his while she sobbed. When she sighed and relaxed in his arms, he carried her back to the bed, tugging the comforter down before easing her inside. "Thank you for sharing your story with me." He kicked his boots off, unsnapped his jeans, pushing them and his briefs down, all while holding Ivy's gaze. "I know how easy it is to look at someone and judge them, making a snap decision about who and what they are. Nobody knows the path that leads them to where they are today. What I do know is, you're more than your past. You see, I saw through the smiles you give me. I knew there was pain hidden behind the mask you wore and still thought you were the most beautiful woman I'd laid eyes on. You never have to hide from me, Ivy."

He moved in next to her, pulling a lock of her hair with his hand.

Ivy moved until she straddled his waist, her fingers tracing the scar he'd covered up with a new tattoo. The roaring lion was mighty and fierce, a symbol he needed at the time.

"You don't ever have to hide from me either," she whispered.

Tymber ran his hands up her legs, his thumbs tracing her outer lips, finding her wet. "I need to be inside you, Ivy."

She laughed, then shocked him speechless as she bent and kissed his chest, tracing the scar with her tongue. "I want you in me too." Her ass wiggled while she moved down, his dick trapped between them slid through her folds.

In that moment, he realized that through tragedy, adversity, and heartache, he'd found his soulmate. With her by his side, he would battle the world to keep her safe from harm.

"I think I love you, Tymber Black," she whispered sliding along his length.

Tymber flipped their positions, leaning over to snatch a condom out of the drawer, he ripped the foil open and had it rolled on in record time. "Good to hear, Ivy, 'cause I'm pretty sure I'm head over ass in love with you as well."

Epilogue

The sound of a Harley pulling up had Tymber looking out the window of his tattoo shop, Twisted Ink. Ember and Lincoln, his two best friends and business partners glanced up as he muttered "Fuck me!" He was sure his tongue had more than likely hit the floor, right along with his tattoo gun at the sight of Ivy climbing off her bike. He stared, mouth agape as she turned her back to his shop, her ass in a pair of tight fitting jeans that molded to her curves like they'd been painted on, while she bent and placed her skull cap on one of her handlebars. Fuck, he wanted to run his hands over every dip and…he pulled his mind away from what he wanted to do with Ivy. Having a major hard-on wouldn't be on his list of things to do in the middle of his shop, especially with Ember and Lincoln staring at him.

He turned to see if they noticed, but both of their eyes were trained on his woman, making him all kinds of irrational. The first thing his caveman instinct wanted to do was punch both men in the nose, rendering their ability to look their fill null and void. The second thing his inner Neanderthal wanted to do, was rush to the door and take her back to his place where he could strip her naked and do all the dirty things he'd fantasized about. Instead, Tymber tossed a balled up bunch of paper toweling toward Ember, who happened to be closest to him, before striding toward the front door to meet Ivy. "Be on your best behavior, assholes," he warned.

"I'm always the best," Ember agreed, wagging his tongue obscenely, his tongue ring glinting in the light.

Lincoln grunted. "You're only the best when I'm not involved, then you're second best. Don't cry like a bitch though, it's hard to compete with all this." Lincoln grabbed his crotch.

Tymber stopped before opening the door, seeing their antics through the reflection in the window. "Nope, not happening. You two are not going to scare her off. She's…special," he breathed.

Ember tossed his hands in the air, the man laying on his table laughed. "Don't even say it, jackass." Ember pointed the tattoo gun toward the guy, silencing him. "Of course she's special, brother. All you've done since you've met her is talk about her. We've been waiting for her to come back ever since you inked her the first time." He crossed his big brawny arms that were covered in tattoos, his emerald green eyes narrowed.

Tymber shrugged but didn't respond right away, his stare going outside. Ivy and he had spent the last few weeks getting to know each other better, solidifying their relationship. He'd known within a very short time she was the woman for him, and she had said the same about him. Shit, she'd fallen asleep under his tattoo gun while he'd been inking her ribs, a spot that was usually tender, yet Ivy had not only not made a peep, she'd fallen asleep, hard.

He pulled the door open but glanced backward. "I know. I'd apologize for not having her come by sooner, but I'd be lying. I didn't want to share our time together just yet."

Lincoln laughed. "You got it bad, boy."

"Oh yeah," he agreed as he walked out meeting Ivy on the sidewalk. "Hey, gorgeous. What're you up to?" Before she could answer, he tugged her into his arms, the need to feel her lips under his overrode all other thoughts. He been sure his caveman instincts were in check. Clearly, he was wrong. If they'd been behind closed doors, he was positive he'd have had the both of them naked, or at least minus enough clothing he could've been buried in her sweet pussy. However, the sound of a car honking brought his head up.

"Hey," she whispered.

He lifted his hand to trace the moisture left on her lips from his kiss. "Hey yourself." Unable to let her go, he kept his arms locked around her waist. "Do you have any clue how fucking sexy you look sitting on your bike, getting off your bike, and hell, even standing next to it? I think I've come up with a dozen fantasies of you and me, fucking on my bike."

She grinned. "Why's it on your bike? I thought you said I was sexy on my bike?"

His right hand trailed down to her ass, cupping one cheek in his palm. "Baby, I'd fuck you on either one of our bikes, but I think my seat is a little bigger, making it much more accommodating for what I have in mind." His dick jerked beneath his denim, letting him know he was more than willing to give it a go. When he'd first met her he had no clue she even owned a bike, yet after finding out she was associated closely with the Royal Sons MC, she had been gifted one years ago by King, the President. Ivy thought, since Luke's death the club would take her bike, the same way they'd taken Luke's. King, being the standup guy Tymber knew him to be wouldn't hear of it.

"Jesus, you make my panties wet just thinking about it." She pressed her forehead against his chest, shivering in his embrace.

Tymber loved how responsive she was to his words and touch. Since the first time they'd made love, she never shied away from whatever he suggested. His girl liked it soft, hard, sweet, or dirty, any way he gave it to her, she enjoyed it.

"Come on inside, I have a couple dickheads wanting to say hi."

Ivy lifted her head. "I came to see if you would ah…give me another tattoo. Remember when we talked about what I wanted?"

His mind raced. One night after they'd made love, she said she wanted to get another tattoo, this one she wanted to see about doing something like the semi-colon, only making it personal. When he'd realized the significance, his mind began working on designs for the suicide symbol, and how he could personalize it for her.

"Yeah, I have a couple drawings for you, but if you don't like them I can start over." He brushed his lips over hers again, unable to stop himself. "Come on, let's take a look." He took a step back, keeping one arm around her.

Ivy looked at the shop next door. "High Maintenance? I've heard of that salon. One of the Old Ladies goes there. I really need a new stylist. Maybe I'll stop in there one day." She nodded toward the closed shop with the colorful window front.

"They're usually open. Not sure what's up." Tymber held the door open to his shop, the familiar buzz of the tattoo guns filling the air.

"Yo, Ivy, you ready to leave him for me yet?" Lincoln asked, not looking up from the woman he was tattooing.

Lux snorted. "Sure, she'll leave the good one for the bad seed."

"That hurts. Come kiss it better." Lincoln scooted back and spread his legs.

"Pretty sure that's sexual harassment." She pretended to write a note in the air. "Keeping notes, boss man," she said without heat.

Lincoln grinned. "I really like the way that rolls off your tongue. I want to hear it when you…"

Lux held her hand up. "If you finish that, I will come over there and staple your lips shut." She held the stapler up, making it click together.

"I'm not into that kind of shit, that's Ember's gig." He pointed his free hand at the other man.

Ember raised his head, eyes narrowed. "You're just jealous. Besides, how do you know if you'd like it or not if you ain't tried it? Am I right?" He asked the room at large.

The woman lying on Lincoln's table laughed. "I think you're all nuts, but then again, I'm lying here getting a tattoo by my ex's enemy so it's all relative."

Silence fell on the entire room.

"Um, who is your ex?" Lincoln asked.

She turned her head, meeting his blue gaze. "Tommy Pelosi."

The name didn't mean shit to Tymber, but it had Lincoln freezing, his usual friendly gaze hardening. "What the fuck are you doing in my shop?"

"Tommy and I got divorced yesterday. I wanted to do something…for myself and this was something he forbid me to do."

Lincoln pushed away from the table, running his hand down his face. "What? Get a tattoo, or get a tattoo from me? 'Cause either one would put you

152

in the shit house with him. Fucking Pelosi's woman."

"Man, you gonna be able to finish, or you need me to come in clutch?" Ember asked.

"Nah, I just finished. I was just getting ready to clean her up." He took a deep breath.

Tymber looked at Ivy then at the woman. "Give me a minute?"

Ivy nodded.

"Here, let me take care of that," he offered, holding his hand out for the solution bottle that they used to spray on a tattoo before wiping away the excess ink. Lincoln shook his head, holding the bottle tighter.

"I got it. Lux, this one's on me. Can you print the aftercare instructions out for Mrs. Pelosi please?" His tone was neutral, the same one he used on clients he didn't know.

Tymber and Ember stayed close, not because they didn't trust Lincoln, but because he was their brother, maybe not in blood, but by choice. They'd been through war together. Lost other brothers in countries they didn't belong, and stayed strong, stayed best friends. Whatever was going down, had gone down before they knew one another, wouldn't change their dynamics.

"I'm sorry, I shouldn't have said anything. This…this was my taking back something he took from…never mind. Thank you for this." She waved at her thigh.

The piece his friend had done was a work of art and had gone up almost to the woman's panty line. If her ex ever sees it, it would mean he was up close and personal to her private parts.

"It's a beautiful piece. Too bad you got it for revenge," Lincoln said, getting up and walking away.

Lux came over to the woman. "Here you go. Now, let me explain to you about aftercare."

Tymber looked to the back, then at Ivy. Shit, he didn't want to leave Link in a fucked up state. They all had demons they fought. He knew more than anyone how screwed up things could get.

"I got this." Ember stood up; his hands no longer covered in gloves. The man he'd been tattooing was shrugging into a T-shirt. "I'll see you in about six to eight weeks for your next session, man. That tat is looking fucking bad ass."

"You're a genius, Ember." He handed over some cash, walking out without looking back.

Lux held the door open for the woman and man, then she strode toward the back following Ember, leaving Tymber with Ivy.

"Well, that was quite the shitshow," Tymber said, coming to stand between Ivy's legs where she sat on the bed.

She looped her arms over his shoulders. "I liked seeing how you all were ready to jump in to back your friend."

He wrapped his arms around her waist, pulling her in snug with his body, loving how she automatically wrapped those long legs of hers around his hips. "He's my brother," he said simply.

155

Ivy gave a little tug, bringing his head down to hers. "You're sexy when you get all protective." She nipped at his lips.

He groaned. "You're sexy when you breathe."

"Ah, you two gonna get nekkid and do it on the table? Asking for a friend," Ember said, strolling into the room while tossing an apple in the air. He caught it in one hand, then bit into it, letting juice run down his chin.

"You're such a voyeur," Lux muttered.

"And?" Ember asked.

"Just pointing out an observation." Lux moved back to her spot at the front of the store. "But, if you two are going to do it, I suggest you wipe that table down really good, you never know what might've spilled on there. I think Ember may have slept there...and had a naughty dream earlier." She moved her hand up and down in a jack off motion, then made as if an explosion occurred, sound effects and all.

"I did no such thing. Take it back," Ember hollered, his apple half eaten sticking out of his mouth making the words garbled.

"Link, was Ember snoring and moaning on Tymber's station earlier this morning?" Lux asked.

Tymber turned to see his other best friend stop in his tracks, looking at Ember, then Lux, then him, his bottom lip getting trapped between his teeth. "Listen, I'm not one to tell a lie, so I'm just gonna go and clean up my station. I'm done for the day."

"I rest my case." Lux did her jackoff motion and explosion imitation again, making Ember toss the apple core toward her, before he growled fuck you.

"You sure you want me to tattoo you here? I can take my kit back to my place and do it there?" The thought of inking her where a bed was close, and no spectators had him itching to reach for his keys.

"Alright, I'm out," Ember announced. "Don't mourn my leaving, I'll see you both tomorrow or the next day. I'm sure, I'll see you before either of you miss me." Ember leaned over Tymber and kissed Ivy on the cheek, jumping backward to avoid Tymber punching him.

"Lock up," Lux said, strolling out after the other two, leaving Tymber and Ivy alone.

"Fuck, I didn't think they'd ever leave." He ran a finger down her cheek, wiping away the trace of Ember, at least in his mind.

"Hmm, whatever shall we do now?" She leaned into his touch.

Tymber looked toward the huge front windows and the passing cars. "Hold that thought." He went through the motions of closing up, locking the door and pulling the huge gate across, then realized her bike sat out front. "Let's move your bike out back. We have a private entrance where we all park."

Ivy hopped down, hurrying to move her bike around. He finished locking up, meeting her at the back door, his tattoo equipment already in the apartment, ready for him to use. "Come on," he said, taking her hand.

The small apartment they kept wasn't anything extravagant, but it was comfortable, fitted with the thought of big men in mind. He led Ivy through the door, engaging the security system. "Did you decide on which design you wanted?" he asked once they were settled at the dining room table.

Ivy pointed at the design that had the sugar skull incorporated with the semi-colon design. He was going to add it to the words he'd already inked onto her ribs, making it the ending to her words. Only it wasn't the ending to her story, rather a new beginning.

"Will you be able to do a sugar skull that small?" she asked, looking at the design.

Tymber raised a brow. "I won't be putting a lot of filigree into the design, but enough to make the skull feminine and you. You trust me?"

Ivy's heart was beating a mile a minute. She absolutely trusted Tymber with her everything. Why this man, when no other man had tripped her trigger, she had no idea. However, from the moment she'd seen him standing in the crisis center hallway, she'd known she could count on him for anything. Like his name, Tymber, he was as sturdy as the strongest trees in the forest. Unlike her name, which she'd hated growing up. Ivy, like a vine, she never wanted to be clingy. Yet he seemed to like it when she wrapped herself around him. "I do. I trust you." And she did.

"If I fuck it up, you can tattoo me. Deal?" Tymber's deep voice rolled over her, making her nipples hard points beneath her shirt.

She laughed. "Trust me, you don't want me anywhere near you with a tattoo gun. You'd have a bunch of squiggly lines, or probably just one squiggly line that resembled an image of sperm. Have you seen what those look like? You'd be the laughingstock of the tattoo industry," she sighed. "No, it's best for you to stick with the art, while I stick with what I'm good at."

She hadn't thought she'd be good at anything until Luke and Darian had encouraged her to follow her dreams. Now, she was glad she had so she didn't have to rely on the MC for her bread and butter. A chick as a mechanic, and hopefully she had enough of a reputation as a good one her business wouldn't be hurt now that she wouldn't be working on the Sons shit.

"Hey, what're you thinking?" Tymber sat her down in a chair, getting down on one knee in front of her.

Ivy bit her lip, wondering how this gorgeous man was still single. "I'm amazed no woman has snapped you up." Her hand flew up and covered her mouth. "Oh shit, forget I said that."

He chuckled, pulling her hand away from her face. "Trust me, I needed a little housebreaking. I think you're just the woman for that job."

Her face had to be ten shades of red. "I suck at this…relationships," she blurted.

Tymber shook his head. "Nah, you just hadn't found the right man. Neither had I. Well, I hadn't found the right woman. You and me, I think we were just waiting for each other." He kissed her palm, placing it over his heart.

"What if I fuck up. What if we fight, or this thing fades?" She waved her hand between them.

He grabbed her other hand, standing up, pulling her with him. "Listen to me. Relationships change, but when two people care about one another the way I care about you and hopefully the way you care about me, then we'll be fine. Better than fine, 'cause we'll be together."

"You said you liked the fire in me. What if…what if my spark dulls?" There it was, her biggest fear.

Instead of answering right away, he lifted her into his arms, and sat down in one of the chairs with her in his lap. "Ivy, I know you think if you fail, or you fall down, nobody will be there to pick you up, right? Well guess what, sweetheart. First thing you need to know is that I'll be right here by your side, ready and willing to help you, but I also know, you'll never lose your spark. Yes, you might

162

stumble and fall, and if you lose your spark, you'll rise back up and you'll be the whole damn fire."

She sniffed; a tear rolled down her cheek. "That's so damn beautiful."

"No, you're so damn beautiful. You and everything about you is. Now, you ready for that tattoo?"

Ivy wiggled, trying to get up without looking like a fool. "I'm ready, but not for the tattoo, not yet anyway." She lifted the hem of her shirt over her head, leaving her in the bra and jeans. A deep inhale could be heard from Tymber, but she didn't stop, wanting to be naked and in his arms. Her riding boots were next, followed by the jeans, which weren't as easy to shimmy out of. Last, she slipped her thumbs into the side of her panties.

"Wait," Tymber barked.

She paused with her thumbs on her hips under the elastic sides. "What?" she asked, tipping her head to the side.

He twirled his finger.. "Turn around, I want to see your ass as you take them off."

Her mouth went dry looking at him with his legs sprawled out in front, his right hand massaging his dick through the denim. "You want me to turn around and—take them off with my back to you?"

"Mmhmm," he murmured.

Fuck, that was one of the sexiest sounds coming from him in that deep guttural command. She turned, her hair swishing along her back.

"Spread your legs a little and bend down as you push them to the floor," he instructed.

Her body ached to have him touch her. The flimsy material was soaking wet already. She inched the sides down, taking her time to ease the silk fabric down, bending like he'd told her to do at the waist, keeping her legs locked so her ass was in the air. A growl was her only warning before she felt his hands on her ass, spreading the cheeks and then his fingers were there, followed by his lips and tongue. "Keep your head down while I have my snack."

Holy shit, holy shit, she chanted in her head. She gripped her ankles, holding herself steady as he worked her up to a hard fast orgasm, screaming his name. "Tymber, oh god, I can't stand," she gasped. Her legs shook from the pleasure.

His arms holding her were the only things that kept her upright, and then he was easing her onto his thighs, his huge cock pressing into her. She didn't know when he'd undressed, only knew she was glad to see she wasn't the only one so affected by her teasing.

"Goddamn, woman, do you have any clue how much I love you?" he asked, his fingers twisted in her hair, turning her face to the side to meet his lips as he pumped his hips upward.

Ivy moaned, her body working to take all of him into hers. "Half as much as I love you?" she teased.

Tymber bit her lower lip, then soothed it with his tongue. "Wrong answer, baby. You're my everything. I used to be glad I woke up and would say just one more day. It was one of the things that kept all of us going. Now, being here with you, balls deep in you, I know I'd fight anything to be right here. We can't let the past ruin our future. Because we didn't give up, we woke up and said fuck you, our journey isn't over, we're here, together. For that alone, I thank my lucky stars." With every word he powered in and out, keeping his eyes locked on hers.

"God, I love you Tymber Black, more than I thought I could ever love anyone. You make me whole, make me want to be better."

He stopped moving, lifting her off him, and turning her to face him. "Ivy, if you were any better you'd be a real life angel. Now, shut up and fuck me like you mean it." He pulled her onto his cock, not giving her a chance to respond.

Ivy gasped, the new position had her clit hitting the perfect spot with each push and pull. She used her arms and legs to work her body over his, glad he helped with a firm grip on her hips when her own legs began to shake.

"Yes, right there. Oh faster. Help me, Tymber," she begged.

His fingers dug into her sides, the familiar tingle began in her breasts, working its way down her chest and then exploded throughout her body, squeezing the dick buried inside her. Ivy panted; her voice hoarse from crying out.

Tymber barely held his orgasm back the first time Ivy came, but the second time her little body clamped down on his there was no holding back. His balls drew up, tingles raced throughout his body seconds before he came, hard, coming in Ivy. They'd had the disease talk, both agreeing they didn't want anything between them, and had proof they had clean bills of health. Now, with her body milking him, he truly wouldn't have cared if she hadn't been protected from pregnancy as he wanted everything with her, even the two point three kids, a dog and a house in the hills. Yeah, he had it bad for his sexy little biker chick, but he couldn't see his life without her in it.

"Shit, I really didn't mean to fuck you on the floor of the apartment," he groaned. His legs would pay for the extra workout they'd been given but not one ounce of him regretted it.

Ivy lifted her head from his shoulder, her smile radiant like always. "You don't hear me complaining."

He ran his hands up and down her sides. "You're probably going to have bruises on you."

She shook her head, smiling down at him. "Again. You don't hear me complaining do you? Actually, we could just have them tattooed on me, so you knew where to place them next time." Her eyes twinkled.

Tymber pictured her wearing his permanent fingerprints. "How about we get up and see about your other tattoo first?"

Ivy shimmied on top of him, the slow roll and grind of her body made him shudder. "If you insist."

Life with Ivy was going to be full of twists and turns, bumps and grinds, but there was one thing he knew for certain. It was going to be one hell of a wild ride. Once you find that one person who completes you, who doesn't want to dull your shine, but will do all they can to fan your flame, you grab hold and hold on tight. He was going to hold on so tight, she'd be wearing his fingerprints even when she wasn't with him, but she'd be smiling from ear to ear remembering the pleasure he gave her when she got them.

The End

Read on for a look at King, president of the Royal MCs story!

Thank You

Thank you for reading Royally Twisted I hope you loved it! Did you enjoy meeting Tymber and Ivy? This story has a lot of meaning to me as I lost a member of my family to suicide. My adopted nephew, several years back. I can honestly say even though time has passed it still hurts to think about him. Cancer is something I'm also intimately familiar with, which sucks hairy monkey balls, and it'll never get easier to hear, when you get the news someone you love has. Do with this story I wanted to make my people have a happily ever after while giving a glimpse of how these two issues affected them. I hope you enjoy their story and fall in love with these two broken people who come out of the fire two phoenix's.

I'd love for you to meet Kailani and Traeger, the next couple in my Royal Sons series! Kailani is a fighter and she too has been through her own Hell. Traeger is the exact warrior she needs. And get ready because following this story is King and Ayesha's story in Royally Tempted book 3.

You can also join my Facebook group, Boon's Bombshells, to discuss all things Elle Boon books and see what's going on or coming up in my book world.

Want to stay up to date on upcoming releases in all my series, not just the Ravens of War? Be sure to join my VIP newsletter here. I promise your inbox will be filled with the hottest dominating Alphas and exclusive content.

Now, turn the page to read an excerpt from the book in the Royal sons, Royally Taken, which is up next…

King gave a nod toward Duke, making it clear Ivy and Tymber were to be allowed to leave, relatively unharmed. The sight of her purse and its contents mocking him. "Frog, Groot, front and center." He waited for them to be within striking distance. "You took it upon yourselves to mess with my family. What do you have to say for yourselves?" The entire club had gone silent.

The loss of his little brother Luke only month before still cut like a knife to the gut, but he didn't let it show. Ivy was like family regardless if she'd been fucking his brother or not. Shit, he still wasn't sure how he felt about her little news she'd just blurted. He glanced over at Luke's twin brother Duke, watching his reaction and seeing only anger burn in his dark gaze. Duke was more like him; mean as a rattle snake that's been poked with a stick one too many times, while Luke was the complete opposite, clearly in more ways than one. Fuck, Luke had been into guys and would rather have killed himself than faced him or Duke. He pushed that knowledge to the back of his mind to go over when he was alone.

Frog's hands fisted at his side, while Groot stood as still as a tree as he'd always done.

"Well, don't make me ask again. You won't like the outcome of the evening if you do," he promised. His voice didn't raise, he didn't have to. If King needed to yell, shit would go down and nobody would be left standing he didn't want to be, and the two idiots with their eyes looking anywhere but at him would be the first to fall.

Groot shrugged his shoulders. "We thought it would show our loyalty if we messed up the bastard that made Luke off himself."

Yeah, his brother, his flesh and blood had taken his own life, thinking he had no other choice and that was on him. He was head of his family, not only the MC.

He could hear the sneer in Groot's tone as he said Luke's name. "So what? Finding out my brother lived with a dude changed your mind? You decided to fuck the shithead up and destroy the place my brother called home?"

"He was fucking that prick," Frog defended his actions.

"You went behind my back and took it upon yourselves to take action as a club, then kept information from me. This upsets me, deeply," he sighed and stood to his full six foot three inch height. "Groot, if I told you to get on your knees and suck my dick, or you were out, what would you do?" King waited, crossing his arms over his chest, his leather cut creaking as he moved the only sound in the room.

Groot wiped his mouth with the back of his hand. "Fuck, King, that's not...that ain't right. I don't swing that way, man."

King nodded, then speared Frog with his will. "How 'bout you, Frog?"

Frog shook his head, but he moved forward.

"You see, that right there is why Frog is getting to keep his cut, for now. You on the other hand, Groot, you've disappointed me. Get the fuck out of my sight and leave my property on the table," he ordered, tapping the table with his finger.

"You gonna stay and suck his dick?" Groot snarled, ripping the leather vest off his back, tossing it onto the ground. Everyone in the MC knew there were rules you didn't break, one of them were you never let your club colors touch the ground, ever.

King gave an imperceptible tilt of his head, sighing as Traeger moved out from the darkened corner along with Wheels. The two men grabbed Groot, one clamping down on each arm.

"I thought you knew the rules, Groot? Don't disrespect the club, being high on that list of things to do and not to do. However, it appears you don't give a fuck about any of that, right?" He grabbed the front of Frog's cut, pulling him in close. "What do you think, Frog?"

Frog shook, fear etched on his features, but he had grit. "I think he's wrong. We fucked up, King."

"Fucking pussy," Groot snarled. "You gonna suck his dick just to stay in the club? Fuck that, I didn't sign up to take any dick in my body." He twisted, trying to free himself from Traeger and Wheels, something King knew wouldn't happen until they were told to release him.

"What do you think we should do to him, Frog?" he asked, not taking his eyes off of Groot. Sweat beaded on the other man's brow, but he never lost the look of disgust.

King could've reassured him that no man's lips or dick was coming anywhere near his own dick, but he wanted to see Frog's reaction. "I...I'm not sure. It's not my place to...to tell you what to do."

He released Frog, slapping him on the shoulder. "That's very wise of you. Next time, don't blindly follow where others may lead." King pulled a gun out from the back of his pants, laying it on the table then slid the blade from his boot, all while looking directly at the prospect named Groot. After he placed the knife next to the gun, he waved at the table. "Your choice, Frog, which do I use to teach Groot a lesson, and don't say it's not your place. I know it ain't, it's mine, but I'm asking, so you answer."

Frog looked from the table to Groot, then back at the table. "The knife," he said after clearing his voice, the croak evident in his tone which was why he'd gotten his nickname.

"Excellent choice. I always did enjoy a little knife play." King picked the blade up, the handle fitting perfectly in his palm. "Here you go, Frog. Teach him a lesson."

King met Duke's stare, each of them knowing whatever went down, would be handled inside the club. Frog gripped the knife in his fist, sweat rolled down his temple. Like on automaton, he moved to where Traeger and Wheels held Groot.

"Don't you fucking do it, Frog. We're brothers," Groot snarled.

"The club comes first, Groot. You knew that coming in," Frog muttered.

"That's where you're wrong, Groot. You ain't got no family here. No friends, nothing. You see, when you tossed my property on the ground, you lost any right to call yourself a brother," King said calmly. Hell, he did everything in a calm way. It was how he operated. Most thought he was cold. It was how he kept level.

Frog adjusted his grip on the knife, his fear almost tangible. "Screw you," Groot snarled.

"I'd rather be judged by the guys behind me, than carried out by six to my final resting place." Frog's words had the Sons murmuring in approval as he uttered their oath. He stepped closer to where Groot was held, the knife gripped in his palm so tightly, King could see his knuckles were white.

Duke moved in like lightning, stopping the forward movement of Frog's hand that held the blade. "Good job, kid." Duke expertly took the knife away, holding it out to the side for King to take. "You on the other hand aren't worthy to wipe the shit off my ass let wear our colors," Duke said quietly, he tilted his head, making a jerking motion toward Groot. "Let him go. Don't want him thinking I'm a pussy and only hit a little bitch when he's being held by two big bastards."

As soon as Groot was free, Duke lunged at him. King watched as his younger brother lashed out, hitting the other man solidly in the chest. He followed him down to the concrete floor, his fist striking Groot several times before he stood. "Some think I'm crazy, that we're crazy. Newsflash, fucker, we are. The difference between us and you, other than the obvious, is we enjoy every second of our insanity. Oh, and if you think to spill any club insights to anyone, we'll know, and then there'll be nowhere you can run or hide from us." Duke pointed at King. "You think what I just did is bad, next time he'll be the reaper and you won't get to walk away, feel me?"

Traeger helped Groot to his feet. "Get outta here, boy." He shoved Groot toward the door, the man's plain white T-shirt smeared with his blood a stark indicator of what went down. As Groot walked out, holding his side, King didn't need to see what his brothers outside did. He knew they'd not recognize him in any way. To them, he was dead.

Ayesha tried to stifle her cry. Shit, she'd come to ask for help, but what she found was like nothing she'd expected. Oh, King Royal, the president of the MC was everything she'd heard he was. What made her pause, made sweat pool beneath her breasts, was the lack of caring he paid to what just happened. Her stomach was in knots having watched the VP named Duke beat Groot without so much as disrupting a bit of hair on his head. The two men were, in a word, dangerous. "I should've listened to Quincy," she whispered.

"That would've been smart," a deep voice spoke from behind her, making her scream.

"I wonder what you're doing hiding back here, when I told everyone to clear out?" King's warm breath fanned over her shoulder, making her shiver.

"I...I'm sorry. I came here to ask a...a question, but now I realize that was a mistake. I'll just be on my way," she said with more bravado than she felt.

King sighed; his hand gentle as he turned her to face him. "Little dove, you should've thought of that before you broke the rules."

Ayesha shook her head back and forth. "I don't—what are you doing?" She yelped as he tossed her over his shoulder.

"Sssh, I'm taking us out of the clubhouse while you explain to me exactly what the hell you had planned, and who sent you." King strolled past a smirking Duke, ignoring the look his younger brother tossed his way. "You're in charge while I'm gone. Make sure someone tails that shithead. We don't need the heat coming down on us."

"If you don't let me go, there's gonna be a lot more than you bargained for coming up here. People know where I am." Ayesha tried to reason with him.

The feel of his palm running over her ass reminded her she'd worn a miniskirt, which made her wriggle harder to get free. A sharp slap made her tense. His words doing the same as he told her to *quit fucking moving* in such a deep voice her body instantly heated. Ayesha had never had a man do what King was, taking complete control of everyone and everything around him. "King, I mean, Mr. Royal, listen to me. I needed help, and I heard you guys were the ones to come to."

He froze in mid step. "Wait 'til we get to the big house."

She'd met Chloe several months back when she'd come into her salon for a haircut. They'd ended up talking about hair color because the other girl liked Ayesha's blue and black hombre fade. When she said Chloe said she'd have to ask her boyfriend before she could do something so daring, it had shocked Ayesha since it was the year two thousand and nineteen, but she hadn't mentioned that to the other girl, not wanting to lose a potential client, nor did she want to hurt her feelings. A couple days later, Chloe had called and made an appointment for a cut and color. That had been the beginning of a great new friendship and an eye opening to a world she'd only seen on TV or read about. If Ayesha was being honest, she envied the other girl and what she had as she'd watched her being dropped off by her boyfriend. He walked her into the shop, looked around as if making sure it was safe, his gaze taking in everything and everyone, possession stamping his features. He would then take Chloe into his arms, staking his claim one last time before he left, demanding she call him when she was done. It had taken monumental effort for Ayesha to tear her eyes away from the kissing couple as he devoured Chloe's mouth, while his hands held the other woman's ass, their bodies fused together. Yeah, Ayesha knew without a doubt they'd be getting it on the moment he had Chloe alone, and the other woman would be more than happy when he was done. She'd only fantasized about having a man do those things to her but had never found one who actually could deliver.

Chloe mentioned the club was more than just a biker gang who ran drugs and guns, but helped damsels in distress, Chloe's words. So when Ayesha's little sister came up missing, or rather ran away, she decided to follow her friend after doing her hair. Big mistake. Huge. She was coming to realize her fool hardy plan could now cost her own life, while her sister Tiana would most probably be sold to the highest bidder in a sex trafficking ring in some third world country. A sob left her throat, but she choked back the next one.

Fear was an ugly bitch, but Ayesha couldn't stifle the sensation from working its way through her, making her break out in a cold sweat. "I think I might be sick," she muttered.

"Don't, you won't like me very much if you do."

"I don't like you very much right now anyway," she muttered angrily. At least if she was angry her it kept her from wanting o vomit all over her sexy kidnaper's back.

King chuckled, then they were walking into his house. The door banging shut behind them was like an omen to her. "Alright, you got five minutes to explain, then I'll decide your fate." He lifted her from his shoulder, placing her feet on the floor, his hands spanning her hips kept her steady. It still took her a several second to get her bearings. She glanced around the room, a little surprised to see it looked like a…normal home.

"You've got four minutes now, better start talking." He let go of her but didn't move away.

She wanted to wipe the smirk off his face with a swipe of her palm across the cheek, but her need for his help kept her hands down. "My sister was kidnapped. I need help getting her back." Shit, she sounded like an idiot.

King raised a brow. "Why you telling me, shouldn't you go to the cops?"

Ayesha rolled her eyes. "Don't you think I tried that first? From all intents and purposes, she went willingly, but I know better. I heard you help do this sort of thing…bring home people who are taken. My sister is one of them."

King tilted his head to the side. "What do I get out of this?"

Ayesha barely controlled her instinct to roll her eyes again. "What do you want, a blow job?"

King laughed, the sound louder than the beating of her heart. "Little dove, if I wanted a blow job, I could open the door and whistle. Within minutes I'd have my pick of women willing to let me fuck their face." He held his arm out, palm facing toward the door.

Oh, there was no doubt in her mind he could and had in the past done that very thing. Why did her heart skip a beat at the image of him opening his jeans for some nameless, faceless woman make her angry? She pulled her focus back to her sister and the very real danger she was in. "I would do anything for my sister, even though I know you don't need me to...whore myself out to you. Tell me, what do I need to do to get your help? Get on my knees and beg? Offer you my first born? Give you a million dollars? What?" she begged, desperate for a reaction, her voice rising.

The door opened behind her, but she didn't take her eyes off of King.

He stepped closer, his body heat making her own feel as if she was on fire, or maybe it was her hormones. "Let's start by you telling me a little more about the who told you this story about me being this hero bullshit, hmm?"

Ayesha shook her head. "This was a terrible mistake," she said, her voice too loud. She backed away, inching back from him

King looked over his shoulder, then at her. "I want you to sit down and don't say another fucking word."

"Hey, you don't have the right to order me around. I'm not one of your club...what ever you call them, brothers, bitches, whatever. You have no right—" she yelped out, the air leaving her lungs at the abrupt motion of being pulled against his rock hard chest.

"Little, girl, I have more than just a right. You're in my club. My territory. I'm not only the President, I'm the fucking King. That's not just my name but means I'm the ruler of all you see here, I wear the patch and crown, baby. Push me and I'll gladly gag you, then I'll paddle that fine little ass until you're crystal clear on that subject. Do you understand?"

She tried to put space between them, silently wishing he was some fat weak asshole who didn't actually have the ability to back up his words. "I came to you for help, not to be...be threatened."

King gave a humorless laugh. "Then you shoulda done your research," he said, turning toward the door. "Duke, get your ass in here. I want to know how the fuck she got past Parker and Clown. If there's a hole, I want it found, and I want it plugged, permanently, one way or another. Feel me?"

Ayesha watched as Duke nodded, his eyes the same determined color as his brother. King turned around, pinning her with such a look she wasn't sure what he planned, but there was no mistake. King was in charge, and whoever Parker and Clown were, they were in big trouble for allowing her to slip inside.

<u>Ravens of War</u>
Selena's Men
Two For Tamara
Jaklyn's Saviors
Kira's Warriors

<u>Mystic Wolves</u>
Accidentally Wolf & His Perfect Wolf (1 Volume)
Jett's Wild Wolf
Bronx's Wounded Wolf
A Fey's Wolf
Their Wicked Wolf

<u>SmokeJumpers</u>
FireStarter
Berserker's Rage
A SmokeJumpers Christmas

<u>Iron Wolves MC</u>
Lyric's Accidental Mate
Xan's Feisty Mate
Kellen's Tempting Mate
Slater's Enchanted Mate
Dark Lovers
Bodhi's Synful Mate
Turo's Fated Mate
Arynn's Chosen Mate
Coti's Unclaimed Mate

<u>Miami Nights</u>
Miami Inferno
Rescuing Miami

Standalone
Wild and Dirty, Wild Irish Series

SEAL Team Phantom Series
Delta Salvation
Delta Recon
Delta Rogue
Delta Redemption
Mission Saving Shayna
Protecting Teagan

The Dark Legacy Series
Dark Embrace

The Royal Sons MC Series
Royally Twisted
Royally Taken, Coming November 2019
Royally Tempted, Coming November 2019

About Elle Boon

Elle Boon is a USA Today Bestselling Author who lives in Middle-Merica as she likes to say…with her husband, her youngest child Goob while her oldest daughter Jazz set out on her own. Oh, and a black lab named Kally Kay who is not only her writing partner but thinks she's human. She'd never planned to be a writer, but when life threw her a curve, she swerved with it, since she's athletically challenged. She's known for saying "Bless Your Heart" and dropping lots of F-bombs, but she loves where this new journey has taken her.

She writes what she loves to read, and that's romance, whether it's about Navy SEALs, or paranormal beings, as long as there is a happily ever after. Her biggest hope is that after readers have read one of her stories, they fall in love with her characters as much as she did. She loves creating new worlds, and has more stories just waiting to be written. Elle believes in happily ever afters and can guarantee you will always get one with her stories.

Connect with Elle online, she loves to hear from you:

www.elleboon.com

https://www.facebook.com/elle.boon

https://www.facebook.com/Elle-Boon-Author-

1429718517289545/

https://twitter.com/ElleBoon1

https://www.facebook.com/groups/RacyReads/

https://www.facebook.com/groups/188924878146

358/

http://bit.ly/2HtHWtsBombshells

https://www.goodreads.com/author/show/812008

5.Elle_Boon

https://www.bookbub.com/authors/elle-boon

https://www.instagram.com/elleboon/

http://www.elleboon.com/newsletter/

Made in the USA
Middletown, DE
07 November 2019